Harbor Of Whispers

Fiction

Alexis Jones

Published by Alexis Jones, 2024.

This is a work of fiction. Similarities to real people, places, or events are entirely coincidental.

HARBOR OF WHISPERS

First edition. January 27, 2024.

Copyright © 2024 Alexis Jones.

ISBN: 979-8224992294

Written by Alexis Jones.

Table of Contents

The Northshore Academy of Martial Arts Dojo crew. You were there when I was younger and I don't know if I would be at the place I'm at now. You guys have been my rock in the past and I love the dojo. Thank you for being there for me when I was younger and being there for me now.

Alexandru Jociva, Thank you for being a great sensei and always believing in me. If it weren't for you, I don't know if this would be possible. You have helped me through so much and continue to be there for me.

Matthew Hibbeler, Thank you for being there when I need you. We may have our ups and downs, but there is always something between us that is unbreakable. These past few years have been wonderful and I love being with you. Thank you for helping me with this book, and many more to come. There is always going to be us, and I appreciate everything you have done. I love you so much and I don't know where I would be without you.

Chapter 1: Arrival

The coastal town of Eldenport was a haven of tranquility, nestled between rolling hills and the rhythmic embrace of the sea. Sophie Mitchell, a journalist yearning for solace from the ceaseless chaos of her city life, arrived at the town's outskirts with a heart heavy with anticipation. The air, thick with the scent of salt and the distant echoes of seagulls, seemed to carry promises of forgotten stories and untold mysteries. As Sophie navigated the narrow streets lined with charming cottages and weathered storefronts, the town's maritime charm wrapped around her like a familiar embrace. The cobblestone paths led her to the heart of Eldenport, where the looming silhouette of the abandoned lighthouse stood against the horizon. Its towering frame, now a haunting monument, cast long shadows over the cobbled streets. Her quaint accommodations, a cozy cottage with a white picket fence, welcomed her with a nostalgic charm. As Sophie settled in, the cool breeze carried whispers of tales etched into the town's history—stories of love, loss, and a lighthouse that stood as both witness and guardian. In the town's only café, Sophie met Oliver Reynolds, a young artist with tousled hair and eyes that seemed to harbor secrets. They struck up a conversation over steaming mugs of coffee, the clinking of cups mingling with the gentle hum of conversation around them.

"Oliver," Sophie inquired, "what can you tell me about the abandoned lighthouse? It seems to hold a certain mystique."

Oliver's eyes flickered with a mixture of curiosity and caution. "The lighthouse has a history, a tale that intertwines with the very fabric of this town. Some say it's haunted by the echoes of a love story that ended tragically."

As the sun dipped below the horizon, casting hues of pink and gold across the coastal sky, Oliver shared tales passed down through generations. He spoke of Thomas and Isabella Morgan, whose love was as boundless as the sea but met a fate as tempestuous as a storm at sea. The town, it seemed, was a vessel holding the echoes of the past, and the abandoned lighthouse stood as a sentinel, silently keeping watch over the untold stories. Intrigued, Sophie decided to embark on a journey through the town's archives, seeking the threads that wove together the narrative of Eldenport. In the flickering lamplight of her cottage, Sophie delved into dusty records, old letters, and fading photographs. The tales of Eldenport's history unfolded before her, like a map leading her through the labyrinth of time. Each document, each artifact, whispered of lives lived and loves lost, leaving an indelible mark on the town. As Sophie's investigation progressed, she discovered a network of connections, hidden beneath the surface of the town's facade. The sea captain, Benjamin Morrison, held fragments of the past in his weathered hands. Evelyn Turner, the bookstore owner, reveled in recounting tales that danced between reality and folklore. Maggie Thompson, an elderly resident, carried the weight of memories as old as the town itself.

The more Sophie uncovered, the more entangled she became in the enigmatic history of Eldenport. The abandoned lighthouse, once a mere silhouette on the horizon, now beckoned her with a promise—a promise of unraveling mysteries, forgotten tales, and the haunting beauty of a town that held secrets as deep as the ocean. As the night wore on, Sophie continued her exploration into the town's past, the glow of her desk lamp casting long shadows on the pages before her. Eldenport, with its tight-knit community and its silent lighthouse, seemed to cradle the whispers of the past, waiting for someone to unravel the threads that bound them together. Little did Sophie know that her journey was just beginning, and the harbor of whispers held more secrets than she could have ever imagined.

The following morning, Sophie woke with a sense of purpose and excitement. The coastal town embraced her like an old friend, the scent of sea breeze wafting through her cottage window. As she stepped into the daylight, Eldenport revealed itself in all its maritime glory. Fishing boats rocked gently in the harbor, and seagulls performed their intricate aerial dances above. She decided to start her day at the local archives, housed in a historic building with weathered bricks and creaking floorboards. The town archivist, Mr. Jenkins, greeted her with a warm smile, his eyes betraying a glint of curiosity. Sophie explained her quest to unearth the history concealed within Eldenport's archives, and Mr. Jenkins guided her to shelves laden with dusty tomes and meticulously organized folders. For hours, Sophie delved into the past, the crinkling of aged paper and the tap of her pen on a notepad the only sounds in the quiet room. Letters between lovers, faded maps, and sepia-toned photographs painted a vivid picture of a town shaped by the ebb and flow of time. She stumbled upon a collection of letters exchanged between Thomas and Isabella Morgan. The words leapt from the pages, vivid and raw, revealing a love story that transcended the constraints of time. The ink on the paper seemed to carry the weight of their emotions—the joy of shared moments, the pain of separation, and the longing for a future that fate had other plans for. As Sophie read, the boundaries between past and present blurred. She could almost hear the distant echoes of laughter and the lapping of waves against the shore. It was as if the spirits of Eldenport's history lingered in the archives, eager to share their stories with a willing listener.

In the afternoon, Sophie emerged from the archives with a treasure trove of information. She found her way to the local diner, a quaint establishment with checkered tablecloths and the comforting aroma of homemade pies. Over plates of freshly caught seafood, she met with Oliver again, eager to share her discoveries.

"Oliver, the letters between Thomas and Isabella are captivating," Sophie began, her eyes alight with excitement. "Their love story is more intricate and poignant than I could have imagined. I want to learn more, to understand the layers of this town's history."

Oliver, who had been sketching on a notepad, looked up with a thoughtful expression. "Sophie, the threads of this town's history are tightly woven. Each person you meet, each story you uncover, contributes to the tapestry of Eldenport. But beware, for not all tales are meant to be unraveled easily. Some secrets, once exposed, may bring both healing and heartache."

The duo continued their conversation, mapping out a plan to approach the locals who held pieces of the puzzle. Sophie felt a renewed sense of purpose as she prepared to immerse herself in the lives of the townspeople, each one a living chapter in the story of Eldenport. As the sun dipped below the horizon, casting a golden glow over the harbor, Sophie and Oliver strolled along the shoreline. The abandoned lighthouse, now a silhouette against the fading daylight, seemed to beckon them with its silent whispers. The journey to uncover Eldenport's secrets had only just begun, and Sophie couldn't help but feel a growing connection to the town—a connection that went beyond mere curiosity. The night descended, and the harbor of whispers embraced them in its quietude, promising more revelations and untold tales in the days to come. Eldenport, with its history veiled in mystery, awaited the unraveling of its secrets by the inquisitive hands of those willing to listen. And in the heart of it all, Sophie Mitchell stood, ready to navigate the currents of the past, guided by the gentle whispers of the coastal town.

The next morning, Sophie embarked on her quest to unravel the town's mysteries by seeking out the key figures she had discovered in the archives. Her first stop was Captain Benjamin Morrison's weathered home, perched on a hill overlooking the harbor. The sea captain greeted her with a twinkle in his eye, as if the ocean's tales were etched into the lines of his weathered face.

"Sophie Mitchell, the journalist in search of Eldenport's secrets," Captain Morrison said with a knowing nod. "Come in, lass. I've been expecting you."

Sophie was captivated as the sea captain shared tales of his seafaring adventures, of storms weathered and distant lands explored. Yet, it was when the conversation turned to the Morgan love story that Captain Morrison's eyes took on a solemn gaze.

"Thomas Morgan, a fine lad with dreams as vast as the open sea. Isabella, his love, anchored him to this town," he recounted. "Their tale is one of passion, but also of tragedy. A love that faced the wrath of the ocean and the fickleness of fate."

As Captain Morrison spoke, Sophie sensed that he held not only the knowledge of Eldenport's history but also a personal connection to the events that had unfolded. The sea captain's tales became a living tapestry, interweaving the grandeur of the sea with the intimate nuances of human emotion. Next on Sophie's list was Evelyn Turner's bookstore, a haven of stories old and new. The jingling of a bell announced Sophie's entrance, and Evie greeted her with a warm smile, inviting her to explore the shelves lined with worn spines.

"Eldenport's stories are like bookmarks in the history of this town," Evie mused, her eyes sparkling. "The lighthouse is a tale that echoes through generations. A beacon of love and heartbreak."

Sophie listened intently as Evie shared anecdotes and folklore, intertwining fact and fiction in a narrative that seemed to transcend the boundaries of time. In the flickering lamplight of the bookstore, Eldenport's history unfolded like the turning of well-worn pages, each chapter revealing the secrets of those who had come before. With newfound insight, Sophie's journey continued to Maggie Thompson's home, where the elderly resident welcomed her with a cup of tea and stories that spanned decades. Maggie's family had been woven into the fabric of Eldenport since its inception, and she held the threads of history with a delicate reverence.

"The lighthouse is more than a structure; it's a keeper of tales, both joyous and sorrowful," Maggie shared. "The Morgan love story, a cornerstone of our history, has left an indelible mark on this town. But it's not the only story the lighthouse guards."

As the day unfolded, Sophie felt the town opening up to her, like a well-worn journal revealing its most cherished secrets. The people of Eldenport were not just characters in a tale; they were guardians of the town's collective memory, each with a chapter to contribute. The sun dipped below the horizon once again, casting hues of pink and orange across the sky, and Sophie found herself back at her cottage. In the quiet of the evening, she spread out her notes and reflections, feeling the weight of the stories she had collected. The abandoned lighthouse stood tall in the fading light, a silent witness to the unraveling narratives of Eldenport. As Sophie Mitchell prepared for another day of exploration, she couldn't shake the feeling that she was not merely documenting history but becoming a part of it. Eldenport's tales were becoming intertwined with her own, and the harbor of whispers seemed to beckon her further into its depths, promising revelations yet to unfold. The mysteries of the coastal town were like a siren's song, and Sophie, captivated by the enchanting melodies of Eldenport, eagerly awaited the next verse in the ongoing saga of Harbor of Whispers.

As the night settled over Eldenport, Sophie Mitchell sat by the open window of her cottage, allowing the gentle sea breeze to carry the echoes of the day's discoveries. The flickering glow of a candle illuminated the pages of her notes, filled with the tales of love, loss, and the haunting presence of the abandoned lighthouse. She gazed out at the silhouette of the lighthouse, now shrouded in the cloak of night. Its solemn form seemed to invite contemplation, and Sophie found herself lost in thoughts that meandered through the alleys of history. The town had welcomed her with open arms, revealing its secrets in layers, and she felt a growing connection to the place and its enigmatic past. The whispering waves, the creaking of distant ships, and the hushed conversations of the townspeople echoed through the night, creating a symphony of stories that resonated in Sophie's heart. Eldenport, with its mysteries and untold tales, had become a living, breathing entity, and Sophie, the weaver of its narratives. As she extinguished the candle, Sophie reflected on the day's encounters—the sea captain's tales of the open ocean, Evie's blend of folklore and fact, Maggie's familial wisdom—all contributing to the rich tapestry of Eldenport. The abandoned lighthouse, once a silent sentinel, now seemed to pulse with the rhythm of the town's collective heartbeat.

With a sense of fulfillment and anticipation, Sophie Mitchell closed her notebook. The first chapter of her journey had unfolded, and the harbor of whispers held the promise of more revelations, hidden beneath the surface of time. Eldenport had cast its spell, and Sophie was eager to navigate the currents of the past, guided by the lantern light of the abandoned lighthouse. As she drifted into the realm of dreams, the sea breeze carried with it the murmurs of the town, the ghostly whispers of a history waiting to be uncovered. The night cradled Eldenport in its embrace, and Sophie, nestled in the heart of the coastal town, embarked on a sleep filled with visions of tales yet to be told. The first chapter had ended, but the story of Harbor of Whispers had only just begun.

Chapter 2: The Lighthouse's Legacy

The next morning, Eldenport awoke to the soft glow of dawn, and Sophie Mitchell embraced the new day with a sense of purpose. Armed with the insights gleaned from the town's storytellers, she set out to uncover more layers of Eldenport's history. Her journey led her to the local museum, a treasure trove of artifacts that whispered of bygone eras. The curator, Mrs. Carter, welcomed Sophie warmly and guided her through the exhibits. Ancient navigational instruments, weathered ship logs, and maritime relics adorned the halls, each item carrying a silent story of the town's maritime legacy. As Sophie explored, a particular exhibit caught her eye—an old, tattered map showcasing the intricate coastline of Eldenport. Mrs. Carter explained its significance with a gleam in her eyes, "This map, passed down through generations, marks the locations of shipwrecks, trade routes, and hidden coves. It's a testament to the symbiotic relationship between our town and the sea."

Among the markings, one symbol stood out—the lighthouse, a focal point on the map as well as in the collective consciousness of Eldenport. Sophie's fingers traced the lines, realizing that the abandoned structure wasn't merely a physical landmark; it was a navigational beacon woven into the very fabric of the town's identity. Determined to explore further, Sophie ventured to the outskirts of Eldenport, where the abandoned lighthouse stood tall against the backdrop of the sea. The weathered path leading to the structure was lined with wildflowers, a stark contrast to the stoic presence of the lighthouse. As she approached, Sophie noticed a small, weathered plaque at the base of the lighthouse. It bore the names "Thomas and Isabella Morgan" and hinted at the enduring love that had once graced these shores. The sea breeze carried with it a sense of melancholy, as if the spirits of the past lingered around the structure, yearning to share their untold tales.

Nearby, a group of local artists had gathered, capturing the lighthouse's stoic beauty on canvases. Among them was Oliver Reynolds, his paintbrush dancing with a rhythm known only to him. Sophie joined the impromptu artists' circle, and together, they painted the lighthouse in strokes that mirrored the town's collective memories. As the sun reached its zenith, Sophie and the artists took a break, sharing stories and laughter beneath the shade of a nearby oak tree. Oliver, with a twinkle in his eye, began to recount a local legend about the lighthouse.

"They say that on stormy nights, the ghostly apparitions of Thomas and Isabella can be seen dancing on the cliffs, their love transcending the barriers of time," he said, his words adding a layer of mystique to the already haunting tales. The day unfolded with a tapestry of experiences—exploring hidden coves, engaging with local fishermen who spun yarns of legendary catches, and absorbing the timeless beauty of Eldenport's coastal landscape. Sophie found herself entranced by the harmony of the town's past and present, realizing that every resident, every structure, was a chapter in the ongoing story of Eldenport. As evening descended, casting a warm glow over the town, Sophie and Oliver decided to visit the local pub, a gathering place for the community. The lively atmosphere resonated with laughter and the strumming of a guitar, creating a backdrop for the evening's tales. Seated in a corner booth, Sophie and Oliver were joined by a group of locals eager to share their own experiences and memories. Each story added depth to the narrative—the young artist who found inspiration in the lighthouse's solitude, the fisherman who believed in the sea's whispers, and the old sailor who spoke of the town's resilience in the face of storms.

As the night unfolded, Eldenport revealed more of its soul to Sophie Mitchell. The threads of the past, intricately woven into the present, painted a portrait of a town bound by shared history and a collective love for the sea. The abandoned lighthouse, standing as a silent sentinel, seemed to embrace the community with open arms, its enduring light guiding the way through the harbor of whispers. The evening wore on, and the town's stories echoed in Sophie's mind as she made her way back to the cottage. The moon cast a gentle glow over Eldenport, and Sophie, with a heart full of newfound connections. The night air carried with it a soothing melody—a symphony of waves, distant laughter from the pub, and the creaking of boats moored in the harbor. Sophie Mitchell sat by the open window of her cottage, the moonlight casting a soft glow on the pages of her notebook. The stories of Eldenport, both spoken and unspoken, reverberated in her mind.

As she reviewed her notes, a sense of gratitude and awe enveloped her. Eldenport wasn't just a town; it was a living, breathing entity, and Sophie felt like a humble traveler navigating the currents of its rich history. The abandoned lighthouse, with its stoic presence and the whispers of a love story that transcended time, stood as both witness and guardian to the tales woven into the town's fabric. The next morning, Sophie woke to the sounds of seagulls and the gentle lapping of waves against the shore. Determined to dive deeper into Eldenport's enigma, she decided to visit the local archives once again, armed with a fresh perspective and a host of new questions. Mr. Jenkins welcomed her with a knowing smile, recognizing the spark of curiosity in her eyes. Sophie delved into old newspapers, ledgers, and town records, searching for any hidden clues that might shed light on the mysteries surrounding the abandoned lighthouse. Each piece of information added a layer to the narrative, as if the town itself was guiding Sophie on her quest for truth. In the midst of her research, Sophie stumbled upon an old photograph—a black-and-white image capturing a moment frozen in time. The picture depicted a group of residents, young and old, gathered in front of the lighthouse during a summer festival from decades past. In the center of the frame stood a couple, their faces filled with joy and a hint of melancholy.

A chill ran down Sophie's spine as she recognized the figures from the plaque at the base of the lighthouse—Thomas and Isabella Morgan. The photograph spoke of a vibrant moment in Eldenport's history, a snapshot of a love that had once bloomed against the backdrop of the sea. Armed with this newfound revelation, Sophie decided to seek out the remaining pieces of the puzzle. She visited Maggie Thompson, hoping the elderly resident might provide insights into the photograph and the festival captured in time. Maggie, seated in her cozy living room surrounded by mementos of the past, welcomed Sophie with a warm smile. As they pored over the photograph, Maggie's eyes sparkled with memories.

"That summer festival was a celebration of life, of love, and of the enduring spirit of Eldenport," she began, her voice carrying the weight of nostalgia. "Thomas and Isabella were the heart of that celebration, their love story woven into the fabric of the town's collective memory."

As Maggie shared stories of the festival, Sophie sensed a deeper connection between the townspeople and the lighthouse. The abandoned structure, once a mere landmark, now emerged as a symbol of love and resilience. The festival, with its vibrant traditions and shared joy, seemed to infuse the very air of Eldenport with an enduring sense of community. With Maggie's tales echoing in her mind, Sophie set out to capture the essence of the festival that had imprinted itself on the town's soul. She visited the local artisan market, spoke with elders who had attended the festival in their youth, and uncovered old newspaper clippings that chronicled the event's evolution over the years. The more she explored, the more Sophie realized that the festival was a reflection of Eldenport's resilience—a celebration that endured despite the passage of time, much like the love story of Thomas and Isabella Morgan. The threads of the past, intricately woven into the present, painted a vivid picture of a town that had weathered storms both literal and metaphorical. As the day turned to dusk, Sophie found herself at the water's edge, staring at the abandoned lighthouse silhouetted against the fading light. The stories of Eldenport, now intertwined with the festival's vibrant history, seemed to resonate in the quietude of the evening. Eldenport, with its abandoned lighthouse, its summer festivals, and the enduring tales of love, became a living storybook, and Sophie Mitchell, the storyteller in search of truth, felt a profound connection to the town and its people. The evening in Eldenport descended with a tranquility that wrapped around Sophie like a comforting shawl. The sea breeze carried a whisper of stories—the ebb and flow of the tides, the distant laughter from the pub, and the gentle creaking of the lighthouse in the quiet of the night. The moon cast its silvery glow upon the coastal town, bathing it in a serene luminance. With the festival's history still fresh in her mind, Sophie returned to her cottage to organize her notes and reflections. The photographs, newspaper clippings, and the tales from Maggie Thompson had unveiled a tapestry of Eldenport's past. As she studied the images captured in black and white, Sophie felt an urgency to delve deeper into the love story that had left an indelible mark on the town.

The following day, Sophie sought out Oliver Reynolds, the young artist whose family held a mysterious connection to the lighthouse. She found him sketching by the water's edge, capturing the play of sunlight on the waves.

"Oliver," Sophie began, "I've learned so much about the festival, about Eldenport's vibrant history. But I can't help but feel there's more to the love story of Thomas and Isabella. Something hidden beneath the surface."

Oliver paused, his eyes reflecting the depths of contemplation. "Sophie, the festival is a celebration, a moment frozen in time. But the love story, it's a river that runs through Eldenport, influencing its course in ways seen and unseen. Perhaps the answers lie not only in the events of the festival but in the everyday moments, the nuances of life."

Intrigued by Oliver's perspective, Sophie decided to explore the everyday aspects of Eldenport—the mundane yet profound moments that shaped the town's character. She visited the local bakery, where the aroma of freshly baked bread mingled with the laughter of patrons The baker, Mrs. Harper, shared stories of generations who had gathered for morning pastries and the timeless conversations exchanged over cups of coffee. As Sophie walked through Eldenport's streets, she encountered small gestures of kindness—a neighbor helping another with their fishing gear, children playing near the harbor, and the rhythmic hum of daily life. Each interaction added another thread to the intricate tapestry that was Eldenport. Her exploration led her to the doorstep of Captain Benjamin Morrison once again. The sea captain, with a weathered logbook in hand, invited her inside. He spoke not only of grand adventures on the open sea but also of the quiet moments in Eldenport that forged unspoken bonds among its residents.

"Eldenport's heartbeat is in the details," Captain Morrison reflected. "The way the sun paints the sky during sunrise, the familiar creak of the dock under your feet, the shared glances between old friends—these are the threads that weave our daily narrative."

Empowered by this realization, Sophie decided to capture these everyday moments through the lens of her journal. She documented the laughter in the pub, the rustle of pages in the bookstore, and the camaraderie among the artists sketching by the lighthouse. In these moments, she discovered a living, breathing Eldenport—a town that thrived not only on the grand tales of its history but also on the quiet symphony of its present. As the sun dipped below the horizon, Sophie once again found herself at the abandoned lighthouse. The sea stretched before her like a vast canvas, and the lighthouse, with its weathered facade, seemed to stand as a sentinel between the threads of time. With the festival and everyday life woven into her narrative, Sophie felt a profound sense of connection to Eldenport. The harbor of whispers had become a treasure trove of stories, each one adding depth to the evolving saga of the coastal town. The night fell, and Sophie, nestled in her cottage, reflected on the day's discoveries. The love story of Thomas and Isabella Morgan, once a distant legend, now resonated within the vibrant fabric of Eldenport's history. The town had welcomed her, embraced her, and in return, she became a weaver of its tales. As the moon cast its gentle glow over Eldenport, Sophie drifted into dreams filled with visions of love, resilience, and the enduring spirit of a town that whispered its secrets in the language of the sea. The night in Eldenport cradled Sophie Mitchell in its gentle embrace as she closed her notebook, filled with the tales of the day. The moon, a silent witness to the unfolding stories, cast its silvery glow over the coastal town, creating a tranquil canvas for reflection.

As Sophie drifted into a peaceful slumber, the sea breeze whispered through her open window, carrying with it the echoes of Eldenport—the festival's joy, the everyday moments, and the timeless love story of Thomas and Isabella Morgan. The harbor of whispers seemed to sigh in contentment, as if acknowledging Sophie's role as a custodian of its secrets. In the quietude of the night, the abandoned lighthouse stood tall against the horizon, a stoic sentinel watching over the town. The threads of Eldenport's history, intricately woven through festivals, everyday life, and love that transcended time, formed a tapestry that fluttered in the sea breeze. As Eldenport settled into the hush of night, Sophie Mitchell, the inquisitive journalist turned custodian of stories, awaited the dawn with a heart full of anticipation. The ongoing tale of Harbor of Whispers promised more revelations, hidden within the folds of the coastal town's past, waiting to be uncovered in the chapters yet to come. The lighthouse's beacon, both a guide and a mystery, flickered with the promise of more secrets and untold whispers in the days that lay ahead.

Chapter 3: The Tapestry Unravels

The dawn in Eldenport painted the sky in hues of rose and gold, a tranquil prelude to the day's discoveries. Sophie Mitchell, fueled by the stories of festivals and everyday life, embarked on the next chapter of her journey through the harbor of whispers. Her footsteps echoed on the cobbled streets as she made her way to the heart of the town. The local bookstore, owned by Evelyn Turner, seemed like the perfect place to gather more threads of Eldenport's rich history. The doorbell jingled as she entered, and Evie welcomed her with a warm smile.

"Sophie, my dear, I've been expecting you," Evie said, her eyes gleaming with a twinkle of anticipation. "The tales of the festival have stirred the echoes of Eldenport's past, haven't they?"

Sophie nodded, eager to delve even deeper. "Indeed, Evie. But now, I want to explore the whispers that may lie beneath the surface—stories that may have faded with time, waiting to be rediscovered."

Evie's bookstore, with its shelves laden with books both new and weathered, held secrets waiting to be unveiled. Together, they perused forgotten volumes and aged manuscripts, unearthing snippets of Eldenport's history that had long been overlooked. In a dusty corner, Sophie found an old leather-bound journal. Its pages, yellowed with age, contained the handwritten musings of a resident from decades past. The author, a fisherman named Samuel Dawson, chronicled his observations of the sea, the changing seasons, and the quiet moments in Eldenport. As Sophie read Samuel's entries, a vivid image emerged—a snapshot of Eldenport in a bygone era. The sea, with its rhythmic dance, played a central role in the narrative. Samuel's words painted a portrait of a town intricately connected to the ebb and flow of the ocean, its heartbeat echoing in the whispers of the deep. Driven by this newfound perspective, Sophie sought out the local fishermen who cast their nets in the harbor. The salty air was alive with tales of legendary catches and the camaraderie forged on the open sea. One old fisherman, with a pipe clenched between weathered teeth, spoke of a peculiar phenomenon.

"The sea has its own language, lass," he said, his eyes squinting against the sunlight. "On stormy nights, when the waves crash against the cliffs, some say they can hear voices carried by the wind—whispers of sailors long gone, sharing their tales with the depths below."

Intrigued by the notion of sea-whispered stories, Sophie spent the afternoon at the water's edge, listening to the lullaby of the waves. It was as if the ocean itself held the key to untold narratives, its depths concealing mysteries that beckoned to be explored. As evening descended, Sophie found herself once again at the pub—a gathering place where the tales of Eldenport mingled with the clinking of glasses and the melodies of a local musician. Seated at a corner table, she engaged in conversation with the townspeople, seeking to uncover more layers of the coastal town's narrative. A seasoned sailor named Jack, with a well-worn sea shanty on his lips, shared a peculiar encounter. "I've sailed these waters for decades, and on clear nights, when the moon is high, there's a spot near the lighthouse where the sea seems to come alive. It's as if the whispers of the deep reach out, telling tales that echo through the hull of the ship."

The mention of the lighthouse stirred a familiar curiosity within Sophie. The abandoned structure, with its silent vigil, seemed to hold the key to Eldenport's mysteries. With Jack's story in mind, she decided to return to the looming silhouette on the horizon as the night enveloped the town. The path to the lighthouse, illuminated by the soft glow of lanterns, felt like a journey into the unknown. As she approached, Sophie noticed a subtle change in the air—a hum that resonated through the rocks and cliffs. Standing before the weathered structure, Sophie closed her eyes and let the whispers of the deep wash over her. It was as if the very stones beneath her feet held the tales of sailors, lovers, and the heartbeat of Eldenport itself. The lighthouse, once a beacon of light, now seemed like a gateway to a realm where the threads of time intertwined.

As the night unfolded, Sophie remained at the lighthouse, enveloped in the symphony of whispers that echoed from the sea. The moon cast a silvery glow over the waves, and Eldenport, with its festival celebrations, everyday moments, and the mysteries of the deep, felt like a living, breathing entity. The abandoned lighthouse, with its silent sentinel, stood witness to Sophie's exploration of Eldenport's secrets. The harbor of whispers, now alive with the tales of the sea, promised more revelations in the ongoing saga of Harbor of Whispers. And as the night wore on, Sophie Mitchell, embraced by the haunting beauty of the coastal town, awaited the next chapter of her journey into the heart of Eldenport's enigma. The sea breeze, infused with the whispers of the deep, played a haunting melody as Sophie stood before the abandoned lighthouse. The night had draped Eldenport in a mystic veil, and the moon's silvery glow painted a dreamscape around the silent sentinel. A distant echo of a sea shanty carried on the wind, and Sophie felt an inexplicable connection to the maritime tales woven into the fabric of Eldenport. The lighthouse, with its timeworn bricks and a lantern that had long lost its flame, beckoned her to explore its secrets in the hushed hours of the night. With a lantern in hand, Sophie ascended the spiraling staircase within the lighthouse. The air was thick with a sense of anticipation as the creaking steps echoed through the hollow tower. The higher she climbed, the more she felt enveloped by the stories that clung to the walls, etched into the very stones.

Reaching the top, Sophie pushed open the creaky door that led to the lighthouse balcony. The sight that greeted her was ethereal—a panoramic view of Eldenport under the moonlit sky. The harbor stretched before her, the waves shimmering like liquid silver, and the town below, quiet in its slumber, held the secrets of the night. As Sophie took in the breathtaking scene, the sea seemed to come alive with a symphony of whispers. It was as if the depths below held an ancient conversation, sharing tales that transcended time. The lighthouse, once a guide for ships at sea, now stood as a conduit between the terrestrial and the celestial. In that moment, a realization struck Sophie—Eldenport was not merely a town with a storied past; it was a living entity, pulsating with the rhythms of the sea and the heartbeat of its inhabitants. The abandoned lighthouse, a silent guardian, held the key to unlocking the mysteries that resonated through the coastal town. Descending from the lighthouse, Sophie wandered through the quiet streets, guided by the subtle glow of lanterns and the distant hum of the sea. The whispers of the deep seemed to permeate every corner, revealing tales that eluded the light of day. She found herself at the local pub, where the atmosphere had shifted with the advancing night. The townspeople, gathered in clusters, spoke in hushed tones, sharing stories that transcended the realm of the ordinary. Sophie joined a group of locals, their faces illuminated by the flickering candlelight, and listened to tales that echoed the maritime history of Eldenport. An elderly fisherman named Mr. O'Connor, his eyes gleaming with the wisdom of years spent at sea, recounted a night when the waters roared with a peculiar intensity. "The sea has its moods, lass. It speaks to those who listen," he said, his weathered hands emphasizing each word. "On that night, it was as if the ocean itself was telling tales of shipwrecks, lost treasures, and the spirits that linger beneath the waves."

The group exchanged knowing glances, acknowledging the mystique that surrounded Eldenport's maritime lore. Sophie felt a deep appreciation for the intricate dance between the town and the sea—a dance that unfolded not only in the light of day but in the shadows of the night. As the hours passed, the pub's patrons dispersed, leaving Sophie with a lingering sense of enchantment. The streets, now bathed in the soft glow of lanterns, beckoned her to explore further. She found herself drawn once again to the water's edge, where the moonlight painted silver pathways on the surface of the sea. Near the lighthouse, she encountered Oliver Reynolds, the young artist who had become her companion in this journey of discovery. He stood near his easel, capturing the moonlit reflections on canvas. Without a word, Oliver handed Sophie a paintbrush, inviting her to join him in creating a visual symphony inspired by the whispers of the night. Under the moon's watchful eye, they painted in silence, each stroke of the brush a testament to the stories that lingered in the air. The lighthouse, standing tall against the night sky, became a beacon not only for ships but for the tales that sailed through the ages. As the night deepened, Sophie and Oliver sat by the water, surrounded by the tranquil beauty of Eldenport under the celestial canopy. The sea, now a mirror reflecting the moon's gentle glow, seemed to hold its breath, as if savoring the magic woven into the night.

In the quietude, a distant melody reached their ears—an old sea shanty carried by the wind. The town, with its festival celebrations, everyday moments, and the haunting whispers of the deep, became a symphony of stories, harmonizing with the nocturnal serenade of the sea. Eldenport, with its timeless tales, embraced Sophie Mitchell and Oliver Reynolds as custodians of its secrets. The harbor of whispers, now alive with the magic of the night, promised more chapters yet to unfold in the ongoing saga of Harbor of Whispers. And as the moon held vigil over the coastal town, Sophie and Oliver, bound by the threads of discovery, awaited the dawn of another day filled with the promise of untold narratives and the enchantment of Eldenport's mysteries. The moon hung in the velvety sky, a silent witness to the unfolding mysteries of Eldenport. Sophie Mitchell and Oliver Reynolds, surrounded by the serene beauty of the night, sat by the water's edge, their minds filled with the enchantment of the coastal town. As the sea murmured its timeless tales, Oliver turned to Sophie with a contemplative gleam in his eyes. "Sophie, there's a legend my family has passed down through generations," he began, his voice hushed in the quietude of the night. "It speaks of a hidden cavern beneath the cliffs, a place where the sea and the stories of Eldenport converge."

Intrigued by Oliver's revelation, Sophie felt a surge of excitement. The notion of a hidden cavern, concealing secrets beneath the cliffs, echoed the enigma that surrounded the abandoned lighthouse. Without exchanging words, they decided to embark on a midnight exploration, guided by the moon's ethereal glow. The path to the cliffs led them through narrow alleyways, where shadows played with the flickering lantern light. The night seemed to hold its breath as they approached the rugged coastline, where the waves whispered secrets against the craggy rocks. Beneath the lighthouse, a concealed entrance revealed itself—a worn staircase leading to the concealed cavern below. The air grew cooler as they descended, the sound of waves growing more pronounced with each step. As they entered the cavern, the atmosphere shifted. Glowing bioluminescent algae adorned the walls, casting an otherworldly luminescence. The cavern, illuminated by nature's own light, felt like a secret chamber where the sea and the stories of Eldenport intertwined. In the heart of the cavern, they discovered an ancient mariner's chest, its timeworn surface hinting at untold treasures within. Oliver, with a sense of reverence, opened the chest to reveal a collection of artifacts—faded letters, sea charts, and a weathered journal. The journal, much like the one Sophie had found in the bookstore earlier, bore witness to the maritime tales of Eldenport. It chronicled the exploits of Captain Elias Blackwell, a legendary figure from the town's seafaring past. His entries spoke of uncharted waters, mythical sea creatures, and encounters with ghostly apparitions beneath the moonlit waves. As Sophie and Oliver delved into the journal's pages, they realized that Captain Blackwell's adventures were interwoven with the very fabric of Eldenport's maritime history. The sea, once perceived as a mere backdrop, emerged as a living entity with its own stories to tell.

Excitement surged through Sophie as she read about a fateful night when Captain Blackwell claimed to have heard the voices of long-lost sailors echoing through the depths. The sea, in its ancient language, seemed to carry tales of shipwrecks, love lost to the abyss, and the enduring spirits that lingered beneath the waves. The cavern, with its bioluminescent glow and the treasures within, became a sanctuary of midnight revelations. Sophie and Oliver, captivated by the tales of Captain Blackwell, felt a profound connection to the seafaring legacy that had shaped Eldenport. As they prepared to leave the hidden cavern, a distant sound reached their ears—a haunting melody carried by the wind. The sea shanty, once a mere echo in the night, now seemed to resonate from the very depths they had explored. Eldenport, with its festival celebrations, everyday moments, and the secrets of the deep, had revealed another layer of its mystique. The abandoned lighthouse, standing sentinel on the cliffs above, seemed to nod in acknowledgment, as if inviting Sophie and Oliver to continue their journey into the heart of the coastal town's enigma. The moonlit night held the promise of more discoveries, and as Sophie and Oliver emerged from the concealed cavern, they carried with them not only artifacts from the past but a profound sense of connection to the sea's eternal tales. The journey through the harbor of whispers had taken an unexpected turn, and the ongoing saga of Harbor of Whispers beckoned them further. With the moon as their guide and the sea as their confidante, Sophie and Oliver embraced the midnight revelations that awaited them in the chapters yet to unfold. The coastal town, alive with the magic of the night, held its secrets close, inviting the duo to become stewards of its untold stories. As Sophie and Oliver emerged from the concealed cavern, the moonlit night cradled Eldenport in its tranquil embrace. The sea, now a silent witness to their midnight revelations, whispered its age-old tales against the craggy cliffs. The coastal town, with its festival celebrations, everyday moments, and the secrets of the deep, seemed to exhale a sigh of contentment as if acknowledging the duo's journey into its hidden realms. The abandoned lighthouse, standing sentinel on the cliffs, cast its silent shadow over the rugged coastline, a symbol of the enigma that Eldenport held within. As Sophie and Oliver made their way back through the quiet streets, the echoes of the sea shanty lingered in the air. The night, alive with the magic of the coastal town, held the promise of more discoveries in the chapters yet to unfold.

Back at their cottages, Sophie and Oliver settled into the quietude of the night, their minds buzzing with the tales of Captain Elias Blackwell and the untold mysteries that lay beneath the waves. The sea, in its eternal language, seemed to invite them to become custodians of Eldenport's maritime legacy. Under the moon's watchful eye, Sophie closed her notebook, filled with the midnight revelations of the hidden cavern. The ongoing saga of Harbor of Whispers had taken an unforeseen turn, and as she drifted into dreams, the sea continued its lullaby—a melody that spoke of love, loss, and the enduring spirit of a coastal town that whispered its secrets in the language of the night. The dawn awaited, promising new horizons and the unveiling of further chapters in the enigmatic tale of Eldenport. The harbor of whispers, now steeped in the magic of midnight revelations, held its stories close, ready to share them with those willing to listen. As the first light of dawn painted the sky, Eldenport embraced a new day, and Sophie and Oliver, bound by the threads of discovery, awaited the next adventure in the ongoing narrative of Harbor of Whispers.

Chapter 4: Connections

The dawn arrived in Eldenport with a gentle glow, casting a soft radiance over the coastal town that had become a tapestry of stories. Sophie Mitchell, fueled by the midnight revelations of the hidden cavern, embarked on a new day with a sense of anticipation. As she strolled through the awakening streets, the sea breeze carried the lingering echoes of the sea shanty from the previous night. The town, still draped in the hush of early morning, seemed to hum with the melodies of Eldenport's maritime history. With Oliver Reynolds at her side, Sophie made her way to the local archives, eager to delve into the annals of Captain Elias Blackwell's voyages. Mr. Jenkins, the custodian of Eldenport's history, welcomed them with a knowing smile, sensing the continuation of their quest. Together, they combed through the archives, unearthing maps, navigational charts, and Captain Blackwell's personal logbooks. The tales inscribed in the captain's meticulous handwriting spoke of uncharted waters, mythical creatures glimpsed on moonlit nights, and encounters with the supernatural that left indelible marks on Eldenport's maritime legacy.

As Sophie transcribed the captain's words into her notebook, she couldn't help but feel a connection to the past—a bridge between the seafaring adventures of Captain Blackwell and the present-day mystery of the abandoned lighthouse. The sea, once perceived as a mere backdrop, had become a living canvas, painted with tales that echoed through the ages. Eldenport, with its festival celebrations, everyday moments, and the secrets of the deep, now unfolded as a saga with chapters written by the sea itself. The abandoned lighthouse, standing sentinel on the cliffs, seemed to nod in acknowledgment, its weathered facade holding the secrets of a bygone era. As the morning progressed, Sophie and Oliver decided to visit Maggie Thompson once more. The elderly resident, with her wealth of memories, became a living bridge to Eldenport's past. As they entered Maggie's cozy living room, she greeted them with a knowing twinkle in her eyes.

"Ah, you've been to the archives, haven't you?" Maggie said, her voice carrying the weight of history. "Captain Blackwell's tales are like threads woven into the very fabric of this town. The sea has a way of etching its stories into the hearts of those who sail its waters."

Maggie shared anecdotes of Eldenport's seafaring days, recounting how the town had once been a bustling port where ships set sail for distant horizons. Captain Blackwell, with his adventurous spirit, had been both a navigator and a storyteller, leaving an indelible mark on the town's maritime legacy. Intrigued by Maggie's stories, Sophie and Oliver decided to explore the town's waterfront, where remnants of Eldenport's seafaring past still lingered. They visited the old shipyard, where weathered vessels stood as silent witnesses to the bygone era of maritime trade. The salty air carried the whispers of sailors long gone, and the creaking of the wooden docks seemed to echo with the tales of countless departures and returns. As they wandered through the waterfront, they encountered an elderly sailor named Old Tom, who had spent a lifetime at sea. His eyes, reflecting the vastness of the ocean, held stories untold. Old Tom spoke of the camaraderie among sailors, the thrill of uncharted waters, and the unspoken bond that tied seafarers to the sea itself.

"The sea is a storyteller, lass," Old Tom mused, his gaze fixed on the horizon. "It shares its tales with those who listen, and Eldenport has been a keeper of those stories for generations. Captain Blackwell knew that, and so do you."

Sophie and Oliver, inspired by Old Tom's words, decided to visit the coastal cliffs where the abandoned lighthouse stood sentinel. The path led them through rugged terrain, and as they approached the towering structure, the sea spread before them like a vast canvas. Standing at the base of the lighthouse, Sophie felt a profound connection to the maritime tales that had woven Eldenport's history. The whispers of the deep, the festival celebrations, and the everyday moments seemed to converge at this point, creating a nexus of stories that echoed through eternity. Oliver, inspired by the surroundings, set up his easel and began sketching the lighthouse against the backdrop of the sea. Sophie, captivated by the view, closed her eyes and listened to the echoes of the past carried by the wind. It was as if the very stones beneath her feet held the imprints of sailors, lovers, and the timeless spirit of Eldenport. As the day unfolded, Sophie and Oliver continued their exploration, weaving through the labyrinth of Eldenport's streets. The town, with its hidden corners and ancient landmarks, revealed layers of history that mirrored the ebb and flow of the sea. In the afternoon, they found themselves at the local artisan market, where skilled craftsmen showcased nautical artifacts and handmade treasures. The market, vibrant with colors and the hum of creativity, seemed to encapsulate the essence of Eldenport—a town that celebrated both its seafaring heritage and the artistic spirit that flourished in its embrace. As the sun dipped below the horizon, casting a warm glow over Eldenport, Sophie and Oliver returned to their cottages, their hearts brimming with the stories of the day. The ongoing saga of Harbor of Whispers, now enriched by Captain Elias Blackwell's maritime tales, promised more chapters yet to be written.

As night descended, Eldenport came alive with the symphony of waves, the flickering lanterns, and the whispers of the deep. Sophie Mitchell, the inquisitive journalist turned custodian of stories, and Oliver Reynolds, the young artist with a brush dipped in the colors of Eldenport's soul, awaited the next sunrise with a sense of wonder. The coastal town, with its festival celebrations, everyday moments, and the mysteries of the sea, held its secrets close. The harbor of whispers, now echoing with the tales of Captain Blackwell, invited Sophie and Oliver to become keepers of Eldenport's eternal stories. And as the moon held vigil over the lighthouse, Sophie's notebook, filled with the maritime legacy of Captain Elias Blackwell, became a testament to the ongoing journey into the heart of Eldenport's enigma. The night settled over Eldenport like a velvet cloak, and Sophie Mitchell, in her cottage overlooking the sea, found herself immersed in the maritime tales of Captain Elias Blackwell. The rhythmic lull of the waves seemed to synchronize with the captain's narratives, creating a symphony of stories that echoed through the harbor of whispers. As Sophie transcribed the last of Captain Blackwell's adventures into her notebook, she felt a sense of gratitude for the threads of history that had woven themselves into the fabric of Eldenport. The sea, with its tales of uncharted waters and mythical encounters, had become a living entity, a storyteller in its own right. The morning dawned with a gentle call from the sea, inviting Sophie and Oliver Reynolds to continue their exploration. With the notebook clasped in her hands, Sophie met Oliver at the water's edge, where the coastal cliffs met the rhythmic embrace of the waves.

"Oliver," Sophie said, her voice carrying the weight of the captain's tales, "I believe there's more to Eldenport than we've uncovered. The sea, the lighthouse, and now Captain Blackwell's stories—they're all connected in ways we're only beginning to understand."

Oliver nodded, his eyes reflecting a shared curiosity. "Sophie, Eldenport is a tapestry of moments, a convergence of the past and the present. What if the sea holds not only the echoes of history but also the keys to unlocking the mysteries that linger in the shadows?"

With renewed determination, Sophie and Oliver set out to explore the coastal cliffs, following the undulating path that led to the abandoned lighthouse. The lighthouse, standing sentinel against the azure sky, seemed to beckon them with a silent invitation to ascend its spiral staircase once more. As they reached the balcony, the panoramic view of Eldenport unfolded before them—a town bathed in the morning light, its charm accentuated by the distant cries of seagulls and the scent of salt carried by the breeze. Sophie, captivated by the beauty that surrounded her, felt a deep sense of connection to the coastal town. Oliver, inspired by the view, began sketching the lighthouse against the backdrop of Eldenport waking up to a new day. Sophie, in the presence of the abandoned structure, closed her eyes and listened to the whispers of the sea, the echoes of Captain Blackwell's tales still resonating in her mind. Descending from the lighthouse, Sophie and Oliver decided to visit the local museum, where artifacts from Eldenport's maritime history were displayed. The curator, a knowledgeable historian named Professor Thomas Harland, greeted them with enthusiasm.

"Ah, the seekers of Eldenport's tales," Professor Harland exclaimed, leading them through the exhibits. "Captain Blackwell's legacy is intertwined with the very essence of this town. His adventures, although extraordinary, are but a part of the larger narrative that Eldenport holds."

In the museum's dimly lit halls, Sophie and Oliver discovered relics from Eldenport's seafaring past—ship models, navigational instruments, and personal belongings of the sailors who had once called the town home. The artifacts, carefully preserved, spoke of a time when Eldenport thrived as a bustling port. Professor Harland, sensing their intrigue, guided them to a section dedicated to the abandoned lighthouse. A collection of old photographs, sketches, and handwritten accounts painted a vivid picture of the lighthouse's storied history.

"It's more than a navigational aid," Professor Harland explained. "The lighthouse has been a witness to love stories, maritime adventures, and the passage of time. Its silent vigil has become a symbol of Eldenport's resilience and enduring spirit."

Armed with newfound knowledge, Sophie and Oliver set out to interview Eldenport's long-time residents, seeking perspectives on the lighthouse and its significance in the town's collective memory. Each conversation added a layer to the evolving narrative, revealing personal anecdotes and cherished memories that had become interwoven with the lighthouse's legacy. As the day unfolded, Sophie and Oliver found themselves drawn to Eldenport's maritime district—a labyrinth of narrow alleys lined with nautical-themed shops and artisan studios. The air was infused with the scent of sea salt and the rhythmic sound of craftsmen shaping wood into intricate ship models. At the heart of the district, they discovered a small bookstore with a sign that read "Captain's Quill." Intrigued, they entered the cozy space, where the scent of old books and the soft hum of sea shanties filled the air. The bookstore's proprietor, a wise and gentle soul named Captain Edmund Sterling, welcomed them with a knowing smile. "Ah, seekers of the sea's secrets," he said, his eyes twinkling with a hint of mystery. "Captain Blackwell's tales have stirred the tides of Eldenport's reflections. Perhaps you're ready to dive deeper."

In the corner of Captain's Quill, surrounded by maritime literature and sea-inspired artwork, Sophie and Oliver engaged in a conversation with Captain Sterling. He spoke not only of Captain Blackwell's adventures but also of the mystical connection between the sea, the lighthouse, and the enduring tales etched into Eldenport's essence.

"As the sea has its ebb and flow, so does Eldenport's story," Captain Sterling mused. "The lighthouse, with its silent vigil, is a keeper of not just maritime history but the very soul of this town. Its light guides not only ships but the threads of time that weave our collective destiny."

Inspired by Captain Sterling's insights, Sophie and Oliver returned to their cottages as the sun dipped below the horizon, casting a warm glow over Eldenport. The harbor of whispers, now echoing with the voices of seafarers and the tales of the lighthouse, held its secrets close, ready to reveal more chapters in the ongoing saga.

The night, adorned with stars and the luminescence of the sea, beckoned Sophie and Oliver to the water's edge. As they stood beneath the moonlit sky, the lighthouse's silhouette against the horizon seemed to merge with the timeless narratives that floated on the night breeze. Eldenport, with its festival celebrations, everyday moments, and the maritime mysteries that unfolded like ancient scrolls, became a haven for storytellers. The harbor of whispers, alive with the echoes of the sea and the reflections of the lighthouse, invited Sophie and Oliver to become guardians of its eternal tales. And so, as the moon held its vigil over Eldenport, Sophie Mitchell's notebook, filled with the maritime legacy of Captain Elias Blackwell, became a cherished time in the ongoing chronicle of Harbor of Whispers. The coastal town, with its secrets and revelations, awaited the next dawn, ready to unveil more threads of its enigmatic tapestry.

The moonlit night held Eldenport in its tranquil embrace, and as Sophie and Oliver stood by the water's edge, they felt the echoes of the day's discoveries reverberating through the coastal town. The lighthouse, now a silent sentinel against the night sky, seemed to guard the secrets that Eldenport held within. In the quietude of the night, Sophie's mind swirled with the threads of Eldenport's tapestry—the sea, the lighthouse, Captain Blackwell's tales, and the timeless spirit of the town. There was a sense that they were on the brink of unraveling a deeper mystery, one that transcended the boundaries of time.

As dawn approached, Sophie and Oliver decided to return to the coastal cliffs, where the abandoned lighthouse stood in stoic contemplation. The first light of morning painted the sky with hues of pink and gold, casting a warm glow over Eldenport's silhouette. The duo ascended the familiar path to the lighthouse, their footsteps echoing in the stillness of the early morning. As they reached the balcony, the sea stretched before them, a vast expanse shimmering with the promise of a new day. Oliver set up his easel once more, capturing the first light as it danced on the waves. Sophie, notebook in hand, found herself drawn to the lighthouse's weathered facade. It was as if the structure itself yearned to share its untold stories. In that moment, a gust of wind carried a faint whisper—the ethereal voice of the sea.

Sophie closed her eyes, allowing the sounds of the waves and the distant cries of seagulls to envelop her. It was as if the very air held the keys to unlocking the mysteries that lingered in Eldenport's embrace.

The sea, ever-changing and eternal, seemed to speak through the gentle lapping of waves against the cliffs. Sophie's senses heightened, attuned to the nuances of the maritime melody. It was in this moment of communion with the elements that she felt a subtle shift—an invitation to delve even deeper into the heart of Eldenport's enigma. Descending from the lighthouse, Sophie and Oliver decided to explore the coastal caves that lined the cliffs. Guided by an instinctual pull, they ventured into the shadows, where the sea had carved intricate patterns into the rock over centuries. As they entered a cavern bathed in the soft glow of bioluminescent algae, Sophie felt a tangible connection to the stories that lingered in the air. The walls of the cavern seemed to breathe with the tales of sailors, lovers, and the enduring spirit of Eldenport. In the heart of the cave, they discovered a collection of symbols etched into the rock—a mosaic of maritime imagery that spoke a language all its own. Oliver, captivated by the enigmatic drawings, began sketching the symbols in his notebook.

"These symbols are like a code," Sophie mused, her eyes scanning the intricate patterns. "It's as if the sea has left its mark, a cryptic language waiting to be deciphered."

They decided to consult Professor Harland at the local museum, sharing their findings and seeking his expertise. The professor, intrigued by the symbols, delved into the town's archives and ancient texts, uncovering references to a maritime language used by Eldenport's sailors in centuries past.

"These symbols are part of a maritime lexicon—a language spoken by the sea-faring community that once thrived here," Professor Harland explained, his eyes gleaming with scholarly excitement. "It's a language of navigation, a code passed down through generations. But its true depth remains a mystery."

The revelation added a new layer to Eldenport's narrative. The sea, the lighthouse, and now the ancient maritime language seemed to converge, creating a tapestry woven with threads of history, mystery, and the passage of time. Eldenport, with its festival celebrations, everyday moments, and the symbols etched into the coastal caves, became a living archive of maritime legacy. Sophie and Oliver, now entwined with the town's enigma, realized they were on the brink of unraveling a tale that transcended the confines of the known. As the day progressed, they returned to the coastal town, contemplating the symbols and seeking more insights from the locals. The harbor of whispers, now alive with the echoes of the sea's language, beckoned them to explore further. In the afternoon, they found themselves at Maggie Thompson's home once again. The elderly resident, wise in the ways of Eldenport, listened attentively as they shared their discoveries. Her eyes widened with recognition as she examined the sketches of the symbols.

"You've uncovered the language of the sea," Maggie said, her voice holding a sense of reverence. "This code, passed down through generations, connects Eldenport to the very heart of the ocean. It's a dialogue between the town and the sea, an ancient conversation that echoes through time."

Maggie recounted tales of sailors using the maritime language to navigate treacherous waters, communicate with distant ships, and share the stories of their voyages. The symbols, etched into the coastal caves, were a testament to the enduring bond between Eldenport's seafaring community and the sea itself. As the sun dipped below the horizon, casting a warm glow over Eldenport, Sophie and Oliver returned to the lighthouse. The abandoned structure, with its silent vigil, seemed to take on new significance. The symbols etched into the coastal caves were like whispers carried by the wind, adding a layer of mystique to the ongoing saga. In the fading light, Sophie stood before the lighthouse, her hands tracing the contours of the ancient brickwork. The sea, now a silent confidante, seemed to respond to the echoes of its own language. Oliver, capturing the moment on canvas, felt the pulse of Eldenport's history coursing through his brushstrokes. The night descended over Eldenport, and as Sophie and Oliver stood by the lighthouse, surrounded by the hushed whispers of the sea, they realized that they had become custodians of a tale that transcended the boundaries of time. The symbols etched into the coastal caves held the promise of unlocking Eldenport's ancient dialogue with the sea. The harbor of whispers, now enriched by the language of the ocean, seemed to invite Sophie and Oliver to embark on a journey that bridged the gap between past and present. As they turned away from the lighthouse, a distant echo reached their ears—the haunting melody of a sea shanty carried by the wind. Eldenport, with its festival celebrations, everyday moments, and the maritime mysteries now entwined with the sea's language, embraced the duo as storytellers in a narrative written by the tides. The coastal town, alive with the symphony of waves and the luminescence of the night, held its secrets close. Sophie's notebook, filled with the maritime legacy of Captain Elias Blackwell, became a companion to the symbols that adorned the coastal caves—a guide in the ongoing exploration of Eldenport's enigma. As they returned to their cottages, the moonlight cast long shadows on the cobblestone streets. Sophie and Oliver, fueled by the day's revelations, realized that the threads of history, the sea's language, and the abandoned lighthouse were interconnected strands in the vast tapestry of Eldenport.

Under the celestial canopy, Eldenport awaited the dawn of a new day—a day that held the promise of deeper discoveries, untold stories, and the unraveling of the ancient language that bound the town to the sea. The harbor of whispers, now alive with the language of waves and symbols, invited Sophie and Oliver to continue their journey into the heart of Eldenport's mysteries. And so, as the night settled over the coastal town, the lighthouse stood as a silent witness, and the sea whispered it's timeless tales, Sophie and Oliver embraced the ongoing saga of Harbor of Whispers, ready to weave new chapters into the fabric of Eldenport's ever-evolving narrative.

Chapter 5: The Festival Approaches

The dawn broke over Eldenport, casting a gentle glow that kissed the coastal town awake. Sophie Mitchell and Oliver Reynolds, invigorated by the discoveries of the previous day, set out with a sense of purpose. The symbols etched into the coastal caves, like ancient hieroglyphs, beckoned them to unravel the language of waves that had bound Eldenport to the sea for generations. Their journey led them to Captain's Quill, the quaint bookstore owned by the wise Captain Edmund Sterling. The aroma of old books and the soft hum of sea shanties welcomed them as they entered the cozy space. Captain Sterling, his eyes gleaming with a knowing twinkle, greeted them. "Ah, seekers of the sea's secrets, I sense that Eldenport has revealed more of its enigma to you," he said, beckoning them to a corner filled with maritime literature. Sophie shared the sketches of the symbols with Captain Sterling, who studied them with a keen eye. "The language of waves is a bridge between sailors and the sea," he explained. "These symbols are not just markers; they're a dialogue with the ocean, a way for Eldenport's seafaring community to navigate both the physical and spiritual realms of the maritime world."

As they delved into ancient tomes and sea charts, Captain Sterling unfolded tales of sailors who had used the maritime language to navigate treacherous waters, predict storms, and communicate with distant ships without uttering a word. The symbols, etched into the coastal caves, became an intricate map of Eldenport's connection to the sea's elemental language. Armed with newfound insights, Sophie and Oliver decided to revisit the coastal caves. The morning sunlight filtered through the rugged cliffs as they traced the symbols with their fingertips, as if trying to decipher the whispers encoded in the very stone. Oliver, inspired by the intricate patterns, began sketching the symbols in his notebook. The sea, visible through the cavern's entrance, seemed to pulse with a rhythmic energy—a heartbeat that echoed the timeless language of waves. As they immersed themselves in the exploration, Sophie noticed a sequence of symbols that formed a distinct pattern. It was as if the sea had left them a message, a series of codes waiting to be understood. She documented the findings in her notebook, feeling a sense of urgency to unveil the secrets woven into Eldenport's maritime legacy. Their next destination was the maritime district, where skilled craftsmen showcased their creations inspired by the sea's language. Sophie and Oliver wandered through the labyrinth of alleys, discovering intricate carvings, seafaring artifacts, and even jewelry adorned with the symbols they had encountered. At a small artisan workshop, they met Emma Turner, a master carver with hands weathered by years of sculpting wood into maritime wonders. Intrigued by their quest, Emma shared her knowledge of the symbols, recounting how they were once carved into the bows of ships for protection and luck on treacherous journeys.

"The sea's language is like a guide through the unknown," Emma explained, her hands expertly carving a small replica of a sailing vessel. "These symbols, passed down through generations, carry the wisdom of sailors who entrusted their lives to the ebb and flow of the ocean."

In the late afternoon, Sophie and Oliver returned to the coastal cliffs, where the abandoned lighthouse stood sentinel against the azure sky. The symbols, now imprinted in Sophie's notebook, seemed to resonate with the lighthouse, creating an intricate tapestry that bound together the elements of Eldenport's mystique. As the sun began its descent, casting a warm hue over the coastal town, Sophie and Oliver decided to share their findings with the locals. The harbor of whispers, alive with the language of waves, awaited their voices to echo the maritime tales that had shaped Eldenport. They convened at the town square, where residents gathered for an impromptu gathering. Sophie stood before the crowd, Oliver by her side, and shared the journey into the language of waves—the symbols, the ancient dialogue, and the stories etched into Eldenport's very foundations. The crowd listened with rapt attention as Sophie unveiled the patterns, and a collective murmur of recognition rippled through the audience. Eldenport's long-time residents, many of them descendants of seafaring families, felt the resonance of the sea's language in their very souls. Maggie Thompson, her eyes reflecting a deep connection to the maritime history, stepped forward. "The symbols are not just a code; they're a legacy," she declared. "They speak of the ties that bind Eldenport to the sea, a language passed down through generations. It's time to revive the dialogue and honor the traditions that have shaped our town."

The atmosphere in the town square shifted, and a shared sense of purpose enveloped the community. Sophie and Oliver, with Captain Sterling and Emma Turner, became catalysts for a revival—a resurgence of the language of waves that had defined Eldenport's identity. The evening unfolded with a celebration in the town square. Lanterns flickered in the fading light as locals gathered, eager to participate in the revival of the sea's language. Emma Turner organized a carving workshop, inviting residents to inscribe the symbols onto wooden plaques that would be displayed in the maritime district. Captain Sterling, with his captivating storytelling, recounted tales of Eldenport's seafaring past, weaving the symbols into the narratives of courage, camaraderie, and the indomitable spirit of sailors who had once called the town home. Under the moonlit sky, Eldenport embraced a new chapter—a chapter where the language of waves became a living heritage, spoken not just by the sea but by the hearts of those who cherished the town's maritime legacy. The abandoned lighthouse, standing tall against the night, seemed to radiate a renewed energy, as if acknowledging the revival of the dialogue that had been silent for too long. As the festivities continued, Sophie and Oliver, surrounded by the warmth of Eldenport's community, realized that they had become integral to the ongoing saga of Harbor of Whispers. The language of waves, once hidden in the coastal caves, now resonated through the town, creating a symphony of stories that echoed in the hearts of those who listened.

And so, beneath the moon's watchful gaze, Eldenport's harbor of whispers held a celebration of not just the sea's language but also the resilience, unity, and enduring spirit of a coastal town that had embraced its maritime heritage. The ongoing narrative unfolded, with Sophie's notebook filled not only with the maritime legacy of Captain Elias Blackwell but also with the symbols that now adorned Eldenport's collective memory. As the night deepened, Sophie and Oliver, along with the entire community, looked forward to the dawn of a new day—a day that would bear witness to the continued exploration of Eldenport's mysteries and the language of waves that connected the town to the eternal rhythms of the sea. The celebration in Eldenport's town square continued into the night, the air filled with laughter, music, and the clinking of carving tools against wood. Lanterns adorned with the newly carved symbols flickered, casting a warm glow over the gathered community. The language of waves, once silent, now echoed through the heart of the coastal town. As the festivities unfolded, Sophie and Oliver, surrounded by the vibrant energy of Eldenport's residents, realized that they were witnessing the birth of a maritime revival. The symbols, once hidden in the coastal caves, had become a bridge between generations—a living language that connected the present to the seafaring heritage of the past. Captain Sterling, with his sea-stories, mesmerized the crowd. His voice carried the weight of Eldenport's history as he recounted tales of daring voyages, legendary captains, and the untold mysteries that lurked beneath the waves. The symbols, now engraved on wooden plaques, adorned the maritime district, transforming it into an open-air gallery that celebrated the town's connection to the sea. Emma Turner's workshop became a hub of creativity, where residents of all ages carved symbols onto wooden pieces. Eldenport's youth, inspired by the revival, eagerly joined in, adding their own interpretations to the ancient maritime language. The town, once anchored in the past, now embraced the interplay between tradition and innovation. Maggie Thompson, with a glint of satisfaction in her eyes, spoke to Sophie and Oliver. "You've opened a door to Eldenport's soul," she said. "The language of waves has awakened a spirit that was dormant for too long. This town, with its maritime heartbeat, now beats stronger than ever."

As the night progressed, the sound of sea shanties filled the air, sung by a local band that had crafted a melody inspired by the rhythmic patterns of the symbols. The town square became a dance floor, where residents moved to the tunes of the sea, their steps weaving a tapestry of unity and shared heritage. In the midst of the celebration, Sophie and Oliver found themselves drawn to the abandoned lighthouse. The structure, now bathed in the soft glow of lanterns, stood as a silent witness to Eldenport's transformation. As they ascended the spiral staircase, they could feel the pulse of the town beneath their feet. On the balcony, overlooking the expanse of Eldenport and the shimmering sea, Sophie and Oliver were greeted by the sight of lanterns dotting the coastline. The symbols, carved into wooden panels, reflected the moonlight, creating a luminous path that mirrored the ebb and flow of the tide. Oliver, inspired by the spectacle, set up his easel once more. With swift strokes, he captured the essence of the moment—the lighthouse, the symbols, and the celebration that pulsed through the town. Sophie, notebook in hand, documented the scene, the culmination of their journey into the heart of Eldenport's enigma. As they descended from the lighthouse, the night sky embraced the coastal town in its celestial blanket. The language of waves, now visible in every corner, seemed to have infused Eldenport with a renewed sense of purpose. The following day brought a sense of calm after the jubilant festivities. Eldenport, adorned with symbols that adorned buildings, boats, and even the local tavern, seemed to breathe with a newfound vitality. Sophie and Oliver, accompanied by Captain Sterling, decided to explore the outskirts of the town. Their journey led them to a secluded beach, where ancient rocks bore natural formations resembling the symbols of the sea's language. It was as if Eldenport itself had etched its dialogue with the ocean into the very foundations of its landscape. Captain Sterling, his eyes filled with reverence, spoke, "The language of waves is not confined to symbols alone; it's written in the stones, the wind, and the rhythm of the tides. Eldenport, once a silent keeper of maritime stories, has become a town that speaks the language of the sea with every heartbeat." In the afternoon, the trio visited the local school, where a teacher named Ms. Abigail Foster had incorporated the language of waves into the curriculum. Students eagerly participated in activities that celebrated Eldenport's maritime heritage, creating their interpretations of the symbols and sharing stories of their own families' connections to the sea. The school's walls adorned with maritime artwork, Ms. Foster expressed her gratitude. "The language of waves has become a living lesson for these children," she said. "It's a legacy they will carry with them, connecting them to Eldenport's rich history and fostering a sense of pride in their coastal roots."

As the day waned, Sophie and Oliver decided to visit the coastal cliffs once more. The symbols, carved into the rocks and etched into the very soul of Eldenport, seemed to resonate with a harmonious energy. The sea, visible through the horizon, whispered its approval, and the sun dipped below the edge of the world, casting a warm glow over the town. The evening brought a sense of serenity, and Eldenport, with its symbols aglow, held a quiet acknowledgment of the journey it had undertaken. The harbor of whispers, now alive with the language of waves, awaited the continuation of its ongoing saga. The coastal town, vibrant with symbols, stories, and the enduring spirit of its seafaring community, prepared for a night that would mark the culmination of the maritime revival. Eldenport, once a harbor of whispers, had become a symphony of voices, each symbol and story adding a note to the melodious narrative that echoed through the town. The evening unfolded with a community gathering at the town square. Locals, young and old, gathered beneath the starlit sky. Emma Turner's workshop showcased the myriad creations inspired by the language of waves—wooden sculptures, intricate carvings, and even a mural that depicted Eldenport's connection to the sea. As the community members shared their interpretations, a sense of collective pride enveloped the crowd. Eldenport, now not just a coastal town but a living testament to the language of waves, had united its residents in a celebration of their maritime identity. Maggie Thompson, standing at the heart of the town square, addressed the gathering. "Tonight, we witness the rebirth of Eldenport," she declared. "The language of waves has not only adorned our town with symbols but has also revived the bonds that connect us to the sea. Let this night be a testament to our resilience, our shared history, and the eternal dialogue between Eldenport and the ocean." The symbol-adorned lanterns, now a signature feature of Eldenport's landscape, were lit one by one, creating a mesmerizing pathway through the coastal town. Sophie and Oliver, alongside Captain Sterling and Emma Turner, led a procession toward the abandoned lighthouse. The lighthouse, standing tall against the night, became the focal point of the evening's festivities. Lanterns were hung on its spiral staircase, casting a soft glow that illuminated the symbols carved into its weathered bricks. Eldenport's heartbeat, now synchronized with the language of waves, echoed through the coastal cliffs. On the balcony of the lighthouse, Sophie and Oliver stood alongside Captain Sterling, overlooking the town they had come to love. The symbols, both ancient and newly carved, seemed to shimmer in unison, creating a visual symphony that mirrored the sounds of the sea. Captain Sterling, with a voice that resonated like the tide, spoke to the gathered community. "Eldenport has found its voice—the language of waves, a dialogue that connects us to the sea and to each other. Tonight, as we stand beneath the celestial canopy, let us cherish this moment of renewal, unity, and the enduring spirit that defines our coastal home."

As he spoke, a hush fell over the town square. The sea, visible in the distance, seemed to respond with a gentle lull that echoed the sentiment of the gathering. Sophie, Oliver, and the entire community held their breath, savoring the significance of the moment. In the quietude that followed, a local musician began playing a haunting sea shanty on a violin. The melody, accompanied by the rhythmic sounds of waves, enveloped Eldenport in a timeless embrace. The residents, inspired by the music, began to dance beneath the stars, their movements weaving a tapestry of joy, resilience, and shared heritage. As the night progressed, the celebration continued with stories shared, songs sung, and symbols admired. Eldenport, now illuminated by lanterns and the luminescence of the sea, felt like a beacon—guiding not only ships but also the hearts of those who called it home. Sophie and Oliver, still on the balcony of the lighthouse, observed the joyous festivities below. The language of waves, once hidden in the coastal caves, now echoed through every corner of Eldenport, creating a harmonious chorus that celebrated the town's maritime legacy. In the early hours of the morning, as the celebration began to wind down, Sophie and Oliver descended from the lighthouse. The town square, now adorned with lanterns and symbols, held a serene beauty that mirrored the sea's quietude after a storm. As the first light of dawn painted the horizon, Eldenport basked in the afterglow of the maritime revival. The symbols, now intertwined with the town's identity, stood as guardians of a legacy that transcended time. The harbor of whispers, now a vibrant harbor of voices, awaited the dawn of a new day—a day that would see Eldenport continue its journey into the heart of its mysteries and the language of waves that connected it to the eternal rhythms of the sea. And so, as the first light kissed Eldenport awake, Sophie's notebook, filled with the maritime legacy of Captain Elias Blackwell and the symbols that adorned the town, became a cherished chronicle in the ongoing saga of Harbor of Whispers. The coastal town, vibrant with symbols, stories, and the enduring spirit of its seafaring community, looked forward to the chapters yet to unfold in the tale of Eldenport's enigma. As the first light of dawn embraced Eldenport, Sophie and Oliver, hand in hand, observed the tranquil beauty that enveloped the coastal town. The symbols, now illuminated by the soft glow of the morning sun, seemed to hold the promise of a new beginning—a chapter where Eldenport's maritime identity flourished, and the language of waves continued to resonate through its heart. The townspeople, their spirits still buoyant from the night's celebration, gathered once more in the town square. Maggie Thompson, with a smile that mirrored the town's newfound vitality, addressed the community.

"Eldenport has undergone a remarkable transformation," she proclaimed. "The language of waves has not only revived our connection to the sea but has also strengthened the bonds that tie us together. Let this chapter be a testament to our resilience, unity, and the enduring spirit that defines our coastal home."

As the cheers of the crowd echoed through the cobblestone streets, Sophie and Oliver exchanged glances, their hearts filled with a deep sense of fulfillment. The abandoned lighthouse, now a symbol of Eldenport's revival, stood proudly against the horizon. In the days that followed, Eldenport continued to thrive. The symbols, now integrated into daily life, adorned buildings, boats, and even the local market stalls. The language of waves had become a living heritage, spoken not just in symbols but in the everyday interactions of the townspeople. Sophie's notebook, once a tool for uncovering mysteries, now became a cherished artifact—a testament to the journey into Eldenport's enigma. She and Oliver, embraced by the warmth of the community, became integral parts of the ongoing narrative. As the seasons changed and the coastal town evolved, the symbols endured, etched into the very fabric of Eldenport's identity. The harbor of whispers, now alive with the language of waves, became a beacon for those seeking connection, unity, and the timeless stories that echoed through the sea. And so, beneath the vast expanse of the sky, Eldenport's ongoing saga unfolded—a tale woven with symbols, stories, and the resilient spirit of a coastal town that had embraced its maritime legacy. The language of waves, once hidden in whispers, now spoke boldly through every crashing wave, every creaking ship, and every heartbeat of Eldenport. As the sun set over the horizon, casting a warm palette of colors over the sea, Sophie and Oliver stood on the coastal cliffs, gazing at the symbols that adorned the landscape. The lighthouse, now a symbol of Eldenport's triumph, stood tall against the changing sky. The harbor of whispers, having transformed into a harbor of voices, awaited the future with open arms. Eldenport, united by the language of waves, stood ready to face the mysteries that lay ahead—a town forever entwined with the sea and the timeless echoes of its maritime heritage.

Chapter 6: Unveiling the Truth

In the wake of the maritime revival, Eldenport entered a period of harmonious transformation. The symbols, once hidden secrets, now adorned the coastal town with a quiet dignity. Each day seemed to carry a resonance of the sea, a subtle reminder of the language of waves that had become an inseparable part of Eldenport's identity. As the town settled into its newfound vitality, Sophie and Oliver found themselves deeply integrated into the fabric of Eldenport's community. They became not just observers but active participants in the ongoing story of the coastal town. Sophie continued her exploration of the archives, delving into the maritime history that had shaped Eldenport for centuries. One day, as Sophie sifted through Captain Elias Blackwell's letters and journals, she uncovered a passage that hinted at a hidden chamber within the lighthouse—a chamber said to hold the key to a deeper understanding of Eldenport's enigma. Intrigued, she shared her discovery with Oliver and Captain Sterling.

"We've uncovered the language of waves, but it seems there may be more to Eldenport's tale," Sophie mused, her eyes reflecting a mix of curiosity and anticipation. Captain Sterling, with a knowing smile, nodded. "The lighthouse has always been more than just a sentinel. It's a repository of stories, secrets, and perhaps, a connection to the very heart of Eldenport."

The trio decided to investigate the lighthouse further, determined to unveil the mysteries concealed within its aged walls. As they ascended the spiral staircase, the air seemed to thicken with the weight of untold stories. The symbols, etched into the bricks, became guides leading them to the heart of the structure. Upon reaching the top, Sophie, Oliver, and Captain Sterling discovered a hidden door tucked away in a corner. As they pushed it open, they were greeted by a dimly lit chamber, adorned with symbols that seemed to dance in the flickering candlelight. The room held artifacts from Eldenport's seafaring past—weathered maps, sailor's knots, and an old ship's wheel. In the center, a wooden chest beckoned, its surface marked with the same symbols that adorned the coastal caves.

Oliver, ever the artist, marveled at the scene. "It's as if this room is a sanctuary for Eldenport's maritime legacy," he observed, his eyes tracing the intricate carvings. As they opened the chest, they discovered a collection of artifacts—a logbook filled with accounts of sea voyages, letters exchanged between sailors, and a faded map that hinted at uncharted waters. The room, a hidden archive, held the echoes of the tides that had shaped Eldenport's destiny. Among the artifacts, they found a journal that belonged to Captain Elias Blackwell. The entries spoke of a mystical connection between the lighthouse and the sea—a connection that went beyond the language of waves they had already uncovered.

"The lighthouse is a beacon not just for ships but for the very essence of Eldenport," Captain Sterling mused as he perused the journal. "It seems to hold a connection to the sea's pulse, a dialogue that transcends the physical realm."

As the trio delved deeper into the journal, they uncovered references to a celestial event that occurred once every century—a convergence of the stars that bathed Eldenport in a unique cosmic energy. The symbols, now illuminated in the chamber, were said to come alive during this celestial alignment, revealing insights into the town's maritime destiny. Excitement filled the air as Sophie, Oliver, and Captain Sterling realized that they stood on the brink of another chapter in Eldenport's enigma. The upcoming celestial event, known as the "Tidecaller's Convergence," promised to unveil secrets that had remained hidden for generations. Word of their discovery spread through the town, igniting a spark of anticipation among the residents. Eldenport, once a harbor of whispers, now buzzed with excitement as preparations for the celestial event began. The symbols, now imbued with a renewed significance, became a focal point of the town's decorations. Lanterns adorned with maritime patterns lined the streets, and the symbols, etched onto banners, fluttered in the coastal breeze. Eldenport, united by the language of waves and fueled by the promise of the Tidecaller's Convergence, brimmed with a sense of collective anticipation. As the celestial event approached, Sophie, Oliver, and Captain Sterling delved deeper into the preparations. They consulted with locals who shared tales of past convergences, each recounting the transformative experiences that had unfolded during these rare celestial occurrences. The coastal town, with its symbols aglow and the lighthouse standing sentinel, awaited the convergence of stars that would unveil the next chapter in Eldenport's maritime legacy. The echoes of the tides, now intertwined with the cosmic dance above, beckoned the residents to gather beneath the celestial canopy and witness the unveiling of secrets hidden within the language of waves. As Eldenport prepared for the highly anticipated Tidecaller's Convergence, the atmosphere in the coastal town was charged with a blend of excitement and reverence. The symbols, now adorning every corner, seemed to shimmer with a heightened luminosity, as if acknowledging the cosmic event that awaited them. In the days leading up to the convergence, Eldenport buzzed with activity. Residents engaged in intricate preparations, decorating the town square with celestial-themed banners, crafting lanterns that mimicked the stars, and even incorporating the symbols into colorful murals that adorned the walls of buildings. Sophie, Oliver, and Captain Sterling became the focal point of Eldenport's collective anticipation. Locals sought their guidance, eager to understand the significance of the Tidecaller's Convergence and the potential revelations it held for the town's maritime legacy. The trio, fueled by a shared sense of curiosity, continued their exploration of Captain Elias Blackwell's journal. The entries detailed the observations made during past convergences, describing mysterious phenomena, heightened sea activity, and even glimpses of ethereal symbols appearing in the night sky.

As the night of the convergence approached, Eldenport brimmed with an otherworldly energy. The town square, adorned with symbols and celestial decorations, became a gathering place for residents eager to witness the cosmic spectacle. Lanterns cast a warm glow, and the air was filled with a hum of anticipation. On the eve of the Tidecaller's Convergence, Sophie, Oliver, and Captain Sterling stood atop the coastal cliffs, gazing at the vast expanse of the night sky. The stars, already brilliant, seemed to intensify in their luminosity, as if aligning in preparation for the celestial event. The lighthouse, now a beacon of both maritime history and cosmic connection, stood tall against the backdrop of the night. Its bricks, etched with symbols, appeared to resonate with the energy building in the air. As the clock struck midnight, Eldenport fell into a hushed silence. The convergence of stars began, each celestial body taking its place in the cosmic dance. The symbols, etched into the very fabric of Eldenport's existence, seemed to respond to the celestial alignment. A subtle shift occurred in the night sky. The residents, gathered in the town square, watched in awe as symbols that mirrored those etched in the coastal caves materialized among the stars. It was a celestial language, a cosmic tapestry woven with the threads of Eldenport's maritime history. Sophie, Oliver, and Captain Sterling, standing on the lighthouse balcony, witnessed the unfolding of the celestial spectacle. The symbols, now visible in the night sky, danced in a mesmerizing pattern—a celestial rendition of the language of waves. As the convergence reached its peak, a gentle hum enveloped Eldenport. The sea, echoing the cosmic energy, seemed to pulse in synchrony with the celestial dance. Waves crashed against the coastal cliffs in a rhythmic cadence, as if joining the cosmic chorus that echoed through the town. In the midst of this celestial communion, a vision unfolded before the residents. The symbols, now aglow with an ethereal light, descended from the night sky and began to hover above the town square. It was as if the language of waves had materialized in a tangible form—a celestial manifestation of Eldenport's maritime legacy.

The townspeople, awe-struck by the celestial display, watched as the symbols interacted with one another, creating intricate patterns that told stories of Eldenport's seafaring past. The lighthouse, bathed in the glow of the cosmic symbols, stood as a sentinel witnessing the convergence of the celestial and the maritime. As the last moments of the Tidecaller's Convergence unfolded, the symbols slowly ascended back into the night sky, leaving a trail of stardust in their wake. Eldenport, now bathed in the afterglow of the cosmic event, erupted into applause and cheers. The coastal town, having witnessed the union of the celestial and the maritime, embraced a profound sense of connection. The symbols, once hidden in whispers and coastal caves, had become a living language that spoke not only through the sea but also through the stars. Sophie, Oliver, and Captain Sterling descended from the lighthouse, their hearts filled with gratitude and wonder. Eldenport, having unveiled a new chapter in its enigma, stood as a testament to the enduring dialogue between the town and the vast expanse of the cosmos. The days that followed were marked by a sense of introspection and unity. Eldenport's residents, now deeply attuned to the language of waves and stars, engaged in conversations about the revelations of the convergence. Symbols adorned not only physical spaces but also the conversations and interactions that shaped the fabric of the coastal town. The lighthouse, having played a central role in the cosmic event, became a pilgrimage site for residents and visitors alike. The hidden chamber within, now known as the "Cosmic Archive," held artifacts that attested to the celestial connection woven into Eldenport's maritime legacy. As Eldenport settled into the new chapter unveiled by the Tidecaller's Convergence, Sophie, Oliver, and Captain Sterling found themselves at the heart of ongoing discussions. The symbols, once shrouded in mystery, had become a source of inspiration, guiding the town's endeavors, innovations, and storytelling. And so, beneath the vast expanse of the sky, Eldenport continued its journey into the heart of its enigma. The language of waves, now intertwined with the celestial dialogue, resonated through the coastal town—a symphony of stories, symbols, and the enduring spirit of a community forever connected to the sea and the cosmos. The harbor of whispers, now alive with both maritime and celestial voices, awaited the dawn of each new day.

As the echoes of the Tidecaller's Convergence lingered in the coastal air, Eldenport embraced a renewed sense of purpose and unity. The symbols, now interwoven with both maritime and celestial significance, continued to illuminate the town with a quiet brilliance—a visual reminder of the ongoing dialogue between Eldenport and the vast expanse of the cosmos. In the days that followed the cosmic event, Eldenport's residents found inspiration in the revelations of the Tidecaller's Convergence. The symbols, once symbols of mystery, became beacons guiding the town's endeavors, innovations, and storytelling. Sophie, Oliver, and Captain Sterling became revered figures in Eldenport, their journey into the heart of the enigma leaving an indelible mark on the coastal town. The Cosmic Archive within the lighthouse, now a revered site, drew visitors seeking to understand the intertwining of Eldenport's maritime legacy with the celestial dance above. The language of waves, having expanded beyond the sea and into the cosmic realms, fostered a sense of interconnectedness among the townspeople. Eldenport, once a harbor of whispers, had evolved into a harmonious harbor of voices—voices that spoke through symbols, stories, and the enduring spirit of a community united by the sea and the stars. As the sun dipped below the horizon, casting hues of orange and pink over Eldenport, the townspeople gathered in the town square.

Lanterns, adorned with celestial patterns, flickered in the evening breeze. A sense of gratitude and reverence filled the air. Maggie Thompson, standing at the center of the square, addressed the gathered community. "The Tidecaller's Convergence has shown us that Eldenport's story is not confined to the sea alone. Our symbols, now illuminated by the stars, tell tales that transcend time and space. Let this chapter be a testament to our resilience, our unity, and the eternal dialogue between Eldenport and the cosmos."

The townspeople, with a shared sense of purpose, nodded in agreement. Eldenport, now guided by the dual rhythms of the sea and the stars, looked toward the future with open hearts and a collective understanding of the mysteries that continued to unfold. As the night settled in, Eldenport embraced a serene beauty. The lighthouse, standing tall against the night sky, seemed to whisper tales of both earthly voyages and celestial adventures. Sophie, Oliver, and Captain Sterling, now integral parts of Eldenport's narrative, found solace in the quietude of the coastal town. The symbols, etched into the very soul of Eldenport, continued to glow softly, mirroring the enduring spirit of a community that had embraced its enigma with open arms. And so, beneath the celestial canopy, Eldenport awaited the dawn of each new day—a day that would see the ongoing exploration of its maritime mysteries, guided by the language of waves and the echoes of the tides. The harbor of whispers, now harmonized with both maritime and celestial voices, stood as a testament to the timeless dialogue between Eldenport and the vast expanse that cradled it.

Chapter 7: Bonds Forming

In the wake of the Tidecaller's Convergence, Eldenport found itself in a state of tranquil transformation. The celestial symbols, now an integral part of the town's identity, continued to cast a subtle glow over the coastal landscape. Eldenport's residents, having witnessed the cosmic dance above, approached their daily lives with a newfound sense of interconnectedness and wonder. The town square, once the epicenter of the celestial event, now served as a communal space where locals gathered to share stories, craft symbols, and engage in conversations that echoed with the language of waves. Eldenport, having uncovered the celestial dimensions of its maritime legacy, looked toward the future with open hearts and a collective understanding that there were still uncharted depths to explore. Sophie, Oliver, and Captain Sterling, having become woven into the fabric of Eldenport's narrative, continued their exploration of the symbols and the mysteries they held. The Cosmic Archive within the lighthouse became a place of reflection and inspiration, drawing those seeking to connect with the town's cosmic and maritime heritage. As the seasons unfolded, Eldenport began to embrace a spirit of exploration. The symbols, once confined to the town square and buildings, found their way onto sails, guiding ships into uncharted waters. The sea, now a canvas painted with the language of waves, beckoned adventurers to set sail and discover what lay beyond the familiar horizon. A new generation of Eldenport's youth, inspired by the celestial revelations, took up the mantle of exploration. They embarked on voyages, carrying symbols as talismans, their ships becoming vessels of the ongoing dialogue between Eldenport and the vast expanse of the sea. The coastal cliffs, where the symbols were carved into the rocks, became a place of reflection and inspiration. Locals and visitors alike found solace in the rhythmic crashing of waves, contemplating the timeless connection between Eldenport and the ocean that stretched to the edge of the known world.

One day, as Sophie and Oliver explored the outskirts of Eldenport, they stumbled upon an ancient compass—its needle pointing not just north but also aligning with the celestial symbols etched on its surface. Intrigued, they shared their discovery with Captain Sterling.

"This compass holds the essence of Eldenport's dialogue with the sea and the stars," Captain Sterling remarked, his eyes gleaming with a mix of nostalgia and excitement. "It's a tool that transcends the physical and leads those who dare to venture into the unknown."

The trio, inspired by the discovery, decided to organize an expedition—a symbolic journey that would see Eldenport's explorers set sail to uncharted waters guided by the celestial symbols and the language of waves. The news of the upcoming expedition spread through the town, sparking a sense of anticipation and adventure. As preparations for the expedition unfolded, the symbols took on a new significance. Each sailor crafted their unique interpretation of the symbols, imbuing their sails and ships with a personal connection to Eldenport's maritime legacy. The town square, now a bustling hub of activity, witnessed the birth of a flotilla that would carry the dialogue between Eldenport and the sea into the uncharted realms. The day of the expedition arrived with a sense of excitement and camaraderie. The townspeople gathered in the town square, waving farewell to the sailors as they set sail, their ships adorned with symbols that shimmered in the sunlight. Sophie, Oliver, and Captain Sterling, standing on the coastal cliffs, watched with pride as Eldenport's explorers sailed toward the horizon. The sea, stretching endlessly before them, seemed to whisper tales of undiscovered lands and uncharted territories. The symbols, etched into sails and compasses, danced in the wind—a cosmic invitation to explore the mysteries that awaited beyond the known world. Eldenport, having embraced both the celestial and maritime dimensions of its enigma, stood as a beacon for those who sought to venture into the uncharted. The town square, now a symbol of unity and exploration, echoed with the language of waves—a living testament to the enduring spirit of a coastal community that had embarked on a journey to embrace the mysteries of the unknown. And so, as the expedition sailed into the horizon, Eldenport awaited the tales that would return with the explorers.

As the flotilla disappeared into the distant horizon, Eldenport stood as a proud guardian of the explorers' journey into the uncharted. The town square, now a gathering place for those left behind, retained the echoes of anticipation and hope. Sophie, Oliver, and Captain Sterling, watching from the coastal cliffs, shared a silent moment of reflection.

"They carry with them the essence of Eldenport—the language of waves and the celestial connection," Captain Sterling murmured, his gaze fixed on the vanishing ships.

Oliver, capturing the scene on canvas, nodded in agreement. "It's a voyage fueled not only by the desire to explore but by the very spirit of our town."

The expedition, guided by the symbols and the cosmic energy of the Tidecaller's Convergence, sailed into uncharted waters. The sailors, a diverse group from Eldenport, each brought their unique interpretation of the symbols, creating a colorful tapestry that mirrored the town's maritime identity. Days turned into weeks, and the explorers navigated through the open sea. The symbols on their sails, now weathered by the elements, retained a resilient glow—a reminder of the enduring dialogue between Eldenport and the vast expanse that surrounded it. Back in Eldenport, the town square became a hub of activity as locals continued to engage with the language of waves.

Symbolic workshops flourished, and conversations about the mysteries of the uncharted took center stage. Eldenport's youth, inspired by the expedition, carved new symbols into the coastal cliffs—symbols that echoed with the promise of future explorations. One evening, as Sophie delved into Captain Elias Blackwell's journal, she uncovered passages that hinted at ancient maps and navigational charts guiding sailors to hidden realms. Excitement filled her as she shared her findings with Oliver and Captain Sterling.

"It seems our explorers might uncover more than just the unknown," Sophie remarked, her eyes gleaming with curiosity.

Captain Sterling, a seasoned sailor, nodded. "The sea has a way of revealing both its wonders and its challenges. The symbols, now intertwined with the spirit of exploration, may guide them to places beyond our wildest imaginations."

News of the potential discoveries spread through Eldenport, adding a new layer of anticipation to the ongoing saga. The town, having embraced the Tidecaller's Convergence and the symbols as catalysts for exploration, stood ready to welcome the explorers back with open hearts and a deep sense of connection. Weeks turned into months, and just as the residents of Eldenport began to wonder about the fate of the expedition, a distant sight appeared on the horizon. The flotilla, weathered but triumphant, sailed back into view. The symbols, now infused with tales of uncharted lands, seemed to resonate with a unique vibrancy. As the ships docked in Eldenport's harbor, the townspeople rushed to greet the explorers. Cheers erupted, and tears of joy flowed freely. Sophie, Oliver, and Captain Sterling joined the crowd, eager to hear the tales of the uncharted. The sailors, their faces etched with the experiences of the voyage, disembarked with a sense of accomplishment. They recounted stories of undiscovered islands, strange creatures, and celestial phenomena that mirrored the language of waves. The symbols, imprinted on ancient maps and charts, became conduits for the tales that unfolded during their explorations. Amidst the jubilant crowd, a sailor named Lila approached Sophie, Oliver, and Captain Sterling. In her hands, she held a weathered map adorned with symbols and cosmic patterns.

"We've discovered a place beyond the known world—a realm where the sea and the stars harmonize in ways we couldn't have imagined," Lila exclaimed, her eyes sparkling with the remnants of celestial wonder.

The trio, intrigued by Lila's revelations, gathered around as she unfolded the map. Symbols, now enriched by the stories of the uncharted, guided the eyes of those present, creating a visual narrative that resonated with the enduring spirit of exploration.

"As we sailed into the unknown, the symbols became our guides, unlocking the secrets of the sea and the cosmos," Lila continued. "This map, a testament to Eldenport's dialogue with the unknown, holds the coordinates to a place where the language of waves reaches its purest form."

The revelation sparked a renewed sense of wonder and curiosity among the townspeople. Eldenport, having embraced its identity as a harbor of exploration, stood on the precipice of a new chapter—one that beckoned residents to venture beyond the known and discover the mysteries that awaited in the uncharted. As the sun dipped below the horizon, casting a warm glow over the harbor, Sophie, Oliver, and Captain Sterling stood with the crowd, gazing at the map that held the promise of future voyages. The symbols, now infused with the tales of the uncharted, seemed to echo through Eldenport—a resounding invitation to continue the ongoing dialogue with the sea and the stars. And so, as the celebrations unfolded in the town square, Eldenport embraced the stories of the uncharted—a continuation of the saga that unfolded in the heart of Harbor of Whispers. The language of waves, now expanded to include the cosmic whispers of the unknown, resonated through the coastal town, guiding its residents toward new horizons and untold adventures. Excitement rippled through

Eldenport as the town absorbed the tales of the uncharted lands discovered by the brave explorers. The map, unfolding like a celestial tapestry, held the promise of continued dialogue between Eldenport and the undiscovered realms that lay beyond the known world.

As the news spread, the town square once again became a focal point for discussions and preparations. Eldenport's residents, fueled by the spirit of exploration, eagerly gathered to decipher the symbols on the map and speculate about the mysteries awaiting discovery. Sophie, Oliver, and Captain Sterling found themselves at the center of the unfolding excitement. The trio, having played integral roles in Eldenport's journey thus far, became conduits for the exchange of ideas and dreams. The Cosmic Archive within the lighthouse, once a repository of past mysteries, now brimmed with the anticipation of future tales. The map, a beacon of potential, guided discussions about the next expedition into the uncharted. Eldenport's youth, inspired by the achievements of their predecessors, eagerly volunteered to join the ranks of the explorers. Sailors crafted new symbols, merging the celestial patterns witnessed during the Tidecaller's Convergence with those unveiled in the discoveries beyond the known world. As the expedition plans took shape, Eldenport resonated with a sense of unity and purpose. The symbols, now imbued with the tales of uncharted lands, adorned not only sails and maps but also everyday objects—symbolic artifacts that connected the townspeople to the ongoing dialogue with the sea and the stars. One evening, as Sophie and Oliver strolled through the town square, they encountered a young artist named Elena. Inspired by the celestial revelations and the symbols, Elena had created a mural that depicted the voyage of the explorers into the uncharted.

"It's a visual representation of Eldenport's ongoing dialogue with the cosmos," Elena explained, her eyes reflecting the same spark of curiosity that had ignited the town.

The mural, a vivid tapestry of colors and symbols, became a symbol in itself—a testament to Eldenport's identity as a harbor of exploration and discovery. Locals and visitors alike gathered around, interpreting the mural's intricate details and finding inspiration in the stories it conveyed. As the day of the next expedition approached, Eldenport brimmed with anticipation. The explorers, their ships adorned with symbols old and new, stood ready to set sail into the uncharted. The town square, transformed into a festive hub, hosted a grand send-off celebration. Maggie Thompson, standing before the crowd, spoke with a voice that echoed with pride and hope. "Eldenport has always been a harbor of whispers, but now, it is also a harbor of shouts—a call to explore, to dream, and to uncover the mysteries that linger beyond the horizon."

The sailors, now seasoned by the tales of the first expedition, nodded in agreement. The symbols, etched into their sails and engraved on maps, seemed to vibrate with the energy of a dialogue that transcended time and space. As the ships departed from Eldenport's harbor, the symbols on their sails caught the coastal breeze, creating a symphony of whispers that lingered in the air. The sea, once again a canvas for exploration, beckoned the sailors toward the mysteries of the uncharted. Sophie, Oliver, and Captain Sterling stood on the coastal cliffs, watching the flotilla vanish into the expanse. The map, carried by the explorers, held the coordinates to realms unknown—a cosmic invitation to unravel the secrets that awaited beyond the known world. And so, Eldenport, having embraced its identity as a harbor of whispers and shouts, awaited the return of the explorers with open hearts. The symbols, now an ever-evolving language of waves and stars, resonated through the coastal town, inspiring dreams of uncharted territories and celestial wonders. As the sun dipped below the horizon, casting a warm glow over Eldenport, the symbols continued to shimmer, becoming beacons that guided the town toward a future filled with discoveries, connections, and the timeless dialogue with the sea and the stars.

As the last glimmers of sunlight danced on the horizon, Eldenport embraced the quiet anticipation that lingered in the coastal air. The symbols, now imprinted not only on sails and maps but also on the hearts of Eldenport's residents, continued to whisper tales of uncharted realms and cosmic wonders. The town square, adorned with symbols and murals, retained a sense of unity and purpose. Eldenport's ongoing dialogue with the sea and the stars had become a collective journey—a tapestry woven with the threads of exploration, discovery, and the resilient spirit of a coastal community forever connected to the mysteries that unfolded in its midst. As the townspeople dispersed, the lighthouse stood tall against the night sky, its beacon casting a gentle glow over Eldenport. Sophie, Oliver, and Captain Sterling, now seasoned custodians of the town's enigma, found solace in the quietude of the coastal night. The murmur of the sea echoed through the cliffs, and the symbols, etched into the rocks and embraced by the night, seemed to resonate with the timeless rhythm of Eldenport's maritime legacy. A sense of gratitude filled the hearts of those who called the harbor home, a gratitude for the sea, the stars, and the ongoing journey that awaited in the uncharted. And so, beneath the celestial canopy, Eldenport settled into the embrace of the night—a night that cradled dreams of exploration, connection, and the unveiling cosmos. The harbor of whispers, now attuned to both earthly and cosmic voices, stood at the threshold of a new dawn.

Chapter 8: Ghosts of the Past

As the explorers sailed into the uncharted, Eldenport settled into a rhythm of anticipation and reflection. The town square, now adorned with symbols old and new, became a space where residents gathered to share stories, interpret murals, and speculate about the wonders that awaited the returning flotilla. Sophie, Oliver, and Captain Sterling, having become custodians of Eldenport's maritime legacy, found themselves drawn to the lighthouse. The Cosmic Archive, now enriched with tales from the first expedition, seemed to hum with the echoes of uncharted realms and the cosmic dance witnessed during the Tidecaller's Convergence. One evening, as Sophie delved into the town's archives, she uncovered ancient manuscripts that spoke of Eldenport's connection to celestial phenomena. The symbols, etched onto the pages, seemed to echo the cosmic patterns witnessed during the convergence.

"Could there be a deeper link between Eldenport and the stars?" Sophie mused, sharing her findings with Oliver and Captain Sterling.

Captain Sterling, his eyes gleaming with curiosity, nodded. "The celestial dance has been a part of our town's narrative for generations. Perhaps the symbols hold a key to unlocking not just the mysteries of the sea but also our connection to the cosmos."

Inspired by this revelation, the trio embarked on a journey to decipher the symbols' celestial significance. They consulted with elders and delved into the lore passed down through generations, seeking clues that would unveil Eldenport's cosmic heritage. As the research unfolded, Eldenport's residents joined in the exploration. Symbolic workshops transformed into celestial gatherings, where locals discussed the alignment of stars, the language of constellations, and the potential connections between the symbols and cosmic events. One clear night, with the celestial canopy above shimmering with stars, Eldenport organized its first Celestial Symposium. The town square, bathed in the soft glow of lanterns and celestial patterns, became a space where astronomers, storytellers, and explorers gathered to share their knowledge and speculations. Maggie Thompson, standing at the center, addressed the crowd. "Eldenport has long been a harbor of whispers, but tonight, let us listen to the whispers of the stars. Our symbols, etched into the fabric of our town, may hold the key to understanding our celestial connection."

As the night unfolded, residents gazed at the heavens, tracing the patterns of constellations that mirrored the symbols. Eldenport's youth, inspired by the cosmic dialogue, crafted new interpretations of the symbols that blended seamlessly with the celestial arrangements above. Sophie, Oliver, and Captain Sterling, witnessing the convergence of symbols and stars, felt a profound sense of unity between Eldenport and the cosmos. The lighthouse, its beacon casting a celestial glow, seemed to resonate with the celestial patterns overhead. As the Celestial Symposium continued, a soft hum filled the air. The symbols, now aglow with a celestial radiance, appeared to dance in response to the cosmic energy. Eldenport, once a harbor of whispers, now echoed with the harmonious dialogue between the town and the vast expanse of the night sky. The celestial revelations sparked a renewed sense of wonder and exploration among the townspeople. Eldenport, having unveiled its connection to the stars, stood ready to embark on a new chapter in its cosmic enigma. The following days saw the town square adorned with celestial patterns, lanterns shaped like constellations, and symbols that seemed to mirror the cosmic dance above. Eldenport, now attuned to both the sea and the stars, embraced its dual identity as a harbor of maritime and celestial whispers. Word of Eldenport's celestial revelations spread beyond its borders, attracting astronomers, seekers of cosmic truths, and those drawn to the allure of the enigmatic coastal town. The symbols, once confined to the coastal caves, now became beacons that guided visitors toward the heart of Eldenport's celestial mysteries. And so, as the Celestial Symposium came to an end, Eldenport looked toward the night sky with a renewed sense of purpose. The language of waves, now interwoven with celestial echoes, continued to resonate through the coastal town—a symphony of stories, symbols, and the enduring spirit of a community forever connected to the sea and the stars. The harbor of whispers, now harmonized with both maritime and celestial voices, awaited the dawn of each new day. Eldenport, now fully immersed in the exploration of its celestial heritage, continued to embrace the newfound connection between the symbols and the stars. The town square, transformed into a celestial haven, became a space where residents engaged in stargazing, shared celestial lore, and celebrated the ongoing dialogue between Eldenport and the cosmos. Sophie, Oliver, and Captain Sterling, fueled by their quest for understanding, delved into ancient manuscripts and consulted with celestial enthusiasts who visited Eldenport. The Cosmic Archive, once a repository for maritime mysteries, now expanded to include celestial charts, diagrams, and the evolving interpretations of the symbols' celestial significance. As the trio explored the intersection of Eldenport's maritime legacy and its celestial connection, they uncovered references to a Celestial Observatory—an ancient structure said to be hidden within the town, dedicated to observing and interpreting the cosmic phenomena above. Excitement filled Eldenport as residents rallied together to uncover the Celestial Observatory. Clues embedded in the symbols, along with whispers from the elders, led the townspeople on a collective journey of discovery. The coastal cliffs, adorned with symbols and celestial patterns, became a canvas that hinted at the location of the hidden observatory. One day, as Sophie, Oliver, and Captain Sterling deciphered a particularly intricate set of symbols, they uncovered a map that pointed to a secluded part of Eldenport—the Whispering Hollow. Legends spoke of this mystical place, where the sea and the stars harmonized in a unique symphony. The townspeople, guided by the symbols and the allure of the Celestial Observatory, gathered at the Whispering Hollow. The air, infused with a sense of anticipation, seemed to hum with a cosmic energy. Sophie, Oliver, and Captain Sterling led the way, their journey weaving through the labyrinthine paths of Eldenport's hidden enclaves. As the group reached the Whispering Hollow, the symbols etched into the rocks seemed to glow with a celestial radiance. The residents, their eyes fixed on the skies above, sensed they were standing on the threshold of an ancient cosmic revelation. In the heart of the Whispering Hollow, concealed by overgrown vines and coastal flora, the Celestial Observatory revealed itself. The structure, weathered by time yet resilient in its cosmic purpose, stood as a testament to Eldenport's enduring quest for celestial knowledge. Sophie, Oliver, and Captain Sterling, their hearts pounding with excitement, entered the observatory. The interior, adorned with celestial murals and symbols that mirrored the stars, held a celestial apparatus that allowed for the precise observation of cosmic events. As night descended over Eldenport, the townspeople gathered within the Celestial Observatory. The symbols, now intricately woven into the observatory's architecture, seemed to align with the stars above. Eldenport, a harbor of both maritime and celestial whispers, prepared to witness a cosmic event that transcended the ordinary. The night sky unfolded in a mesmerizing display. Constellations took shape, and the symbols within the observatory responded in kind. The celestial dance mirrored the language of waves, creating a symphony that resonated through the Whispering Hollow. Eldenport's residents, entranced by the cosmic spectacle, shared stories of their own interpretations of the symbols. The observatory, now a nexus of celestial knowledge and community connection, became a space where Eldenport's identity as a harbor of whispers and shouts reached new heights. As the celestial event reached its peak, a subtle hum filled the air. The symbols within the observatory emitted a glow that transcended the physical realm, connecting Eldenport to the vast cosmic expanse. It was a moment of celestial communion, a union between the town and the stars. And so, within the Celestial Observatory, Eldenport discovered not only the hidden depths of its cosmic heritage but also a platform for ongoing exploration and revelation. As the residents exited the Whispering Hollow, their hearts resonated with a profound sense of interconnectedness—a realization that Eldenport, nestled between the sea and the stars, was an eternal part of a cosmic dialogue that transcended time and space. The town square, now aglow with the light of celestial lanterns, became a space for reflection and celebration. Eldenport, having unveiled the Celestial Observatory, stood at the nexus of maritime and celestial exploration. The symbols, now imprinted not only on sails and maps but also within the very fabric of the town, continued to echo through the coastal community. The Celestial Observatory in the Whispering Hollow had become a sanctum for Eldenport's exploration of the cosmic mysteries. As the townspeople gathered within the observatory, their eyes turned toward the night sky, a celestial symphony unfolded, resonating with the language of waves and stars.

Sophie, Oliver, and Captain Sterling, surrounded by the celestial murals and symbols, marveled at the profound connection between Eldenport and the cosmos. The symbols within the observatory seemed to vibrate with an energy that transcended the physical realm, and the air buzzed with the shared anticipation of revelations yet to unfold. As the night progressed, the townspeople engaged in celestial discussions, interpreting the constellations and symbols that adorned the observatory's walls. Eldenport, now fully immersed in the exploration of its celestial heritage, stood on the brink of a new chapter—an odyssey into the depths of cosmic understanding. Within the observatory, Sophie uncovered an ancient tome that spoke of a Celestial Convergence—a rare cosmic event where the stars aligned in a unique pattern, unlocking hidden truths and cosmic wisdom. The symbols within Eldenport, it seemed, were intricately connected to the upcoming convergence. Excitement spread through the coastal town as news of the Celestial Convergence circulated. Eldenport's residents, now attuned to the celestial language, prepared for the imminent cosmic event. Symbolic workshops flourished, and discussions about the convergence's significance filled the town square. As the day of the Celestial Convergence approached, the townspeople gathered within the Whispering Hollow. The Celestial Observatory, aglow with the soft radiance of symbols and celestial patterns, awaited the alignment of stars that would mark the pinnacle of Eldenport's celestial exploration.

Under the night sky, the stars gradually shifted into a unique alignment, mirroring the symbols within the observatory. The air hummed with an otherworldly resonance, and the symbols seemed to come alive, pulsating with an ethereal glow. Eldenport, standing at the precipice of the Celestial Convergence, witnessed a cosmic spectacle unfold. The alignment of stars created a celestial tapestry that reflected the symbols on the observatory's walls, forming a bridge between the town and the cosmic energies that enveloped it. As the convergence reached its zenith, a surge of energy coursed through Eldenport. The symbols, now aglow with celestial radiance, began to resonate with the collective consciousness of the townspeople. Eldenport's connection to the stars transcended the physical, becoming a shared experience that united the community in a cosmic reverie. In the midst of the Celestial Convergence, the symbols within the observatory transformed, revealing hidden layers of meaning. Eldenport's residents, guided by an intuitive understanding of the cosmic language, felt a profound sense of enlightenment—a communion with the celestial forces that had shaped the town's destiny. Sophie, Oliver, and Captain Sterling, standing at the center of the Whispering Hollow, witnessed the cosmic revelations with awe. The symbols, now infused with the wisdom of the stars, seemed to whisper tales of Eldenport's cosmic heritage—a heritage that reached back through time and connected the town to the very fabric of the universe.

As the Celestial Convergence waned, Eldenport's residents exited the observatory with a newfound sense of clarity. The town square, bathed in the residual glow of the cosmic event, became a space for contemplation and celebration. Eldenport, having unveiled the mysteries of its celestial heritage, stood united as a harbor of both maritime and cosmic whispers. The symbols, now enriched by the Celestial Convergence, continued to resonate through the coastal town. Eldenport, having embraced the ongoing dialogue with the sea and the stars, looked toward the future with open hearts and a deepened understanding of the cosmic forces that shaped its destiny. And so, as the night sky gradually returned to its ordinary state, Eldenport stood at the dawn of a new epoch—a chapter that promised to explore the intersections of maritime and celestial exploration.

As the echoes of the Celestial Convergence gradually faded into the night, Eldenport found itself bathed in a quiet luminescence—a residual glow that lingered in the air. The symbols within the Celestial Observatory, having revealed hidden layers of meaning, stood as testaments to the town's enduring connection with the cosmos. Sophie, Oliver, and Captain Sterling, stepping out into the Whispering Hollow, felt a profound sense of gratitude and wonder. The celestial revelations had deepened Eldenport's understanding of its own enigma, uniting the community in a shared cosmic reverie. The town square, now aglow with lanterns shaped like constellations, became a space where residents gathered to share their experiences of the Celestial Convergence. Eldenport's youth, inspired by the cosmic events, began to craft new symbols that blended the maritime heritage with celestial insights, adding another layer to the ongoing dialogue with the sea and the stars. As dawn approached, Sophie, Oliver, and Captain Sterling stood on the coastal cliffs, gazing at the horizon where the sea met the sky. The symbols, etched into the rocks and resonating with the cosmic revelations, seemed to shimmer with a timeless energy—a language that transcended the boundaries of the known world. In the quiet moments before sunrise, Eldenport embraced the dawning of a new day—a day that held the promise of continued exploration, discovery, and the interplay of maritime and celestial whispers

Chapter 9: Unraveling Mysteries

In the wake of the profound Celestial Convergence, Eldenport found itself on the threshold of a celestial odyssey. The symbols, now enriched by cosmic revelations, became not only markers of maritime history but also conduits for ongoing exploration into the mysteries of the cosmos. The town square, adorned with symbols both old and new, became a nexus of celestial discussions and preparations for the next phase of Eldenport's journey. Residents engaged in celestial workshops, crafting intricate symbols that reflected the newfound understanding of their cosmic heritage. Sophie, Oliver, and Captain Sterling, having become stewards of Eldenport's celestial legacy, delved deeper into the Cosmic Archive. Ancient manuscripts hinted at further celestial events and uncharted territories that awaited exploration. The trio, fueled by an insatiable curiosity, set out to uncover the next steps in Eldenport's celestial odyssey. The Celestial Observatory, now a revered space for cosmic contemplation, became a hub of celestial gatherings. Eldenport's astronomers and stargazers, drawn by the allure of the symbols and the cosmic tapestry, engaged in nightly observations, decoding the language of the stars. As the months unfolded, Eldenport prepared for a Celestial Odyssey—an expedition guided not only by the language of waves but also by the celestial whispers that echoed through the symbols. Sailors adorned their ships with new celestial symbols, each one carrying the promise of uncharted realms and cosmic wonders.

One evening, as Eldenport's residents gathered in the town square, Sophie addressed the crowd. "Our journey into the cosmos has just begun. The symbols, now intertwined with celestial insights, beckon us to explore the unknown and unveil the mysteries that linger beyond the horizon."

The announcement sparked a renewed sense of excitement and anticipation among the townspeople. Eldenport's youth, inspired by the prospect of a Celestial Odyssey, eagerly volunteered to join the expedition. The harbor, once a hub of maritime activity, now buzzed with the energy of celestial preparations. Eldenport's ships, adorned with celestial symbols that mirrored the patterns of the night sky, set sail into the open sea. The symbols, etched into the sails and embraced by the sailors, seemed to carry the essence of Eldenport's celestial heritage—a heritage that invited the town to continue its ongoing dialogue with the cosmic forces that shaped its destiny. As the flotilla ventured into uncharted waters, the symbols on the ships vibrated with a celestial resonance. Eldenport, now a harbor of both maritime and cosmic whispers, sailed toward the unknown, guided by the interplay of the language of waves and the stars. Sophie, Oliver, and Captain Sterling, standing on the coastal cliffs, watched the Celestial Odyssey unfold. The symbols, now carried into the cosmic expanse, became beacons that connected Eldenport to the vast celestial canvas above. The sailors, their eyes fixed on the symbols and the night sky, navigated through the sea with a sense of purpose and wonder. The Celestial Odyssey, born from the revelations of the Celestial Convergence, promised not only to unveil uncharted realms but also to deepen Eldenport's understanding of its cosmic identity. And so, as the flotilla disappeared beyond the horizon, Eldenport stood as a harbor of maritime and celestial whispers. The Celestial Odyssey unfolded across the open sea, guided by the celestial symbols that adorned Eldenport's ships. As the flotilla ventured into uncharted waters, the sailors embraced the dual legacy of maritime and celestial exploration. The symbols on their sails, aglow with the cosmic resonance of the Celestial Convergence, seemed to carve a luminous path through the night.

Eldenport's residents, gathered in the town square, continued their celestial observations. Astronomers, storytellers, and those drawn to the allure of the cosmic journey shared their insights, interpreting the celestial patterns that mirrored the symbols. The town, now a harbor of both maritime and celestial whispers, awaited news from the Celestial Odyssey. In the heart of Eldenport, the Cosmic Archive buzzed with activity. Sophie, Oliver, and Captain Sterling, fueled by the ongoing curiosity and the yearning for cosmic knowledge, delved into ancient texts and celestial charts. The symbols, now imbued with the energy of the Celestial Convergence, revealed hints of further cosmic events that awaited discovery.

One clear night, as the Celestial Odyssey sailed into uncharted realms, Eldenport experienced a celestial event known as the Stellar Mirage. The night sky transformed into a breathtaking display of luminous illusions, as if the stars themselves were dancing in celebration of the town's cosmic journey. The townspeople, enchanted by the Stellar Mirage, gathered in the town square. Celestial symbols, etched into lanterns and decorations, twinkled alongside the stars. Eldenport's youth, inspired by the cosmic spectacle, began crafting new interpretations of the symbols that reflected the dance of the stars above. Sophie, Oliver, and Captain Sterling, standing within the Celestial Observatory, observed the Stellar Mirage with awe. The symbols within the observatory responded to the celestial display, creating a harmonious interplay between the town and the cosmic forces that surrounded it. As the Stellar Mirage waned, Eldenport's astronomers noted a subtle shift in the celestial patterns. The symbols on the ships, now aligned with the changing constellations, guided the sailors toward a region where ancient star maps hinted at the presence of a Celestial Archipelago—an archipelago shrouded in cosmic mysteries.

The Celestial Odyssey, propelled by the whispers of the stars and the symbols, reached the outskirts of the Celestial Archipelago.

Eldenport's sailors, their eyes fixed on the celestial patterns above, navigated through uncharted waters guided by a celestial compass. As the ships approached the archipelago, a sense of anticipation filled the air. The symbols, etched into the rocks and embraced by the islands, seemed to resonate with the cosmic energy that enveloped the celestial haven. Eldenport, now standing at the threshold of a new cosmic realm, prepared to unveil the mysteries hidden within the Celestial Archipelago. The sailors, guided by the symbols and the cosmic resonance, explored the islands one by one. Each island held celestial wonders, from ancient observatories that aligned with cosmic events to mystical caves where the symbols seemed to pulse with otherworldly energy. The Celestial Archipelago, it appeared, was a celestial sanctuary—a space where Eldenport's ongoing dialogue with the cosmos deepened. The symbols, now intertwined with the cosmic energies of the archipelago, revealed layers of celestial wisdom that added new dimensions to Eldenport's understanding of its cosmic heritage. And so, as the Celestial Odyssey continued to unfold within the Celestial Archipelago, Eldenport sailed further into the cosmic expanse. The symbols, now woven into the fabric of both maritime and celestial exploration, continued to resonate through the coastal town. As Eldenport's flotilla navigated through the Celestial Archipelago, the symbols on the sails resonated with the cosmic energy that permeated the islands. Each stop revealed celestial wonders and unfolded new chapters in the ongoing odyssey. The sailors discovered ancient celestial observatories, where the symbols aligned with specific constellations, unlocking insights into the cosmic dance. Mystical caves held echoes of celestial chants, and Eldenport's residents, now attuned to the cosmic language, felt a deep connection to the archipelago's celestial realms. The islands themselves seemed to respond to Eldenport's presence, revealing hidden passages and secret chambers adorned with symbols. Sophie, Oliver, and Captain Sterling, leading the exploration, marveled at the interplay of the symbols and the archipelago's celestial energies.

One evening, within a cavernous chamber illuminated by celestial light, the trio stumbled upon an ancient mural. The mural depicted Eldenport's symbols intertwined with cosmic constellations, telling a story of the town's enduring dialogue with the stars.

"Each symbol carries the essence of our connection to the cosmos," Sophie remarked, her eyes tracing the celestial patterns. "They are not just markers of our maritime history but conduits for understanding the celestial forces that guide us."

As Eldenport's sailors continued their celestial voyage, the symbols on the sails began to resonate with a newfound luminosity. The Celestial Archipelago, now a living testament to the town's cosmic exploration, echoed with whispers of celestial revelations. One night, as the flotilla gathered near the heart of the archipelago, a celestial phenomenon known as the Starlight Convergence unfolded. The symbols on the ships, now charged with the archipelago's cosmic energy, responded to the convergence by emitting a radiant glow. Eldenport's residents, witnessing the celestial spectacle from the islands, felt a surge of cosmic energy coursing through the symbols. The convergence became a moment of celestial communion, where the town and the archipelago became intertwined in a dance of starlight and symbols. In the midst of the Starlight Convergence, a celestial portal appeared—a shimmering gateway that seemed to connect Eldenport to celestial realms beyond the archipelago. The symbols, now aglow with celestial radiance, beckoned the sailors to venture through the portal and explore the cosmic territories that awaited. Eldenport, standing at the precipice of the celestial gateway, faced a choice—to embark on a journey into the unknown or to remain within the cosmic embrace of the Celestial Archipelago. The symbols, now pulsating with cosmic energy, seemed to whisper tales of uncharted realms, celestial wonders, and the timeless dialogue that awaited in the celestial expanse.

As the sailors pondered the decision, the celestial portal continued to shimmer, inviting Eldenport to venture into the cosmic unknown. The town square, now filled with the soft glow of celestial lanterns, reflected the cosmic energy that permeated the archipelago. And so, with the choice before them, Eldenport stood at a crossroads of cosmic destiny. The symbols, now charged with the wisdom of the Celestial Archipelago, resonated through the town. The night air in the Celestial Archipelago held a palpable tension as Eldenport's sailors pondered the celestial portal before them. The symbols on the ships, now aglow with the energy of the Starlight Convergence, seemed to pulse with the heartbeat of a cosmic adventure. Sophie, Oliver, and Captain Sterling stood at the forefront of the decision, their eyes reflecting the celestial radiance. The townspeople, gathered on the islands, waited in anticipation, their hearts entwined with the symbols that had become conduits to the celestial forces. In the quiet moments that followed, a consensus emerged among the sailors. The call of the celestial portal resonated with the spirit of exploration that had defined Eldenport's maritime legacy. The decision was made—the Celestial Odyssey would continue beyond the archipelago's boundaries.

The celestial portal, now embraced by the symbols, opened wider, casting a shimmering bridge between Eldenport and the cosmic realms that lay beyond. The flotilla, guided by the symbols and propelled by the whispers of the stars, sailed through the portal with a sense of collective purpose. As the last ship disappeared into the cosmic expanse, the Celestial Archipelago seemed to sigh, its celestial energies harmonizing with the echoes of the Starlight Convergence. The symbols on the islands glowed softly, marking the departure of Eldenport's sailors into the celestial unknown. The town square, bathed in the lingering glow of the convergence, became a space for reflection and celebration. Eldenport's residents, inspired by the cosmic journey, shared stories, and contemplated the cosmic tapestry that now intertwined with the maritime legacy. And so, Eldenport embarked on a new chapter of its celestial odyssey. The symbols, now imprinted not only on sails and maps but also on the very fabric of the town, continued to echo through the coastal community—a resounding invitation to embrace the mysteries that awaited in the ever-unfolding tale of Harbor of Whispers. The harbor of both maritime and celestial whispers stood at the threshold of a cosmic adventure, ready to explore the uncharted territories that lay beyond the celestial portal.

Chapter 10: Confrontations

The celestial odyssey of Eldenport unfolded in a kaleidoscope of cosmic wonders. As the flotilla sailed through the uncharted realms, the symbols on the ships became conduits for a celestial dialogue that resonated with the stars, nebulae, and cosmic energies that surrounded them. Eldenport's sailors, now seasoned celestial explorers, recorded their observations in celestial journals. The symbols, once markers of maritime history, evolved into a celestial lexicon—a language that communicated with the cosmic forces shaping the destiny of the town. One evening, within the heart of a radiant cosmic cluster, Eldenport's astronomers noticed a peculiar alignment of stars. The symbols on the ships responded with an intricate dance, echoing the celestial patterns above. It became clear that Eldenport had reached a Celestial Nexus—a convergence of cosmic energies that held the key to deeper celestial understanding. As the flotilla anchored within the Celestial Nexus, Eldenport's residents gathered on the ships' decks, their eyes fixed on the cosmic spectacle above. Sophie, Oliver, and Captain Sterling, standing at the forefront, sensed a profound cosmic resonance that echoed through the very fabric of the universe. Within the Celestial Nexus, Eldenport's sailors experienced a cosmic communion. The symbols, now attuned to the celestial forces at play, emitted a soft glow that intertwined with the cosmic energies. It was a moment where the language of waves and the whispers of the stars became one—a synthesis of maritime and celestial voices. The cosmic energies within the Nexus revealed fragments of cosmic lore—tales of celestial civilizations, ancient cosmic rituals, and the interconnectedness of celestial realms. Eldenport, now a town transcending the boundaries of Earthly shores, embraced its role as a Celestial Nexus—a meeting point of cosmic energies that invited explorers from all corners of the universe. As Eldenport's sailors delved deeper into the mysteries of the Celestial Nexus, they discovered ancient celestial libraries—repositories of cosmic knowledge etched into celestial structures. The symbols, now carriers of celestial wisdom, seemed to guide the explorers through the cosmic archives, unraveling the secrets of the universe.

The Celestial Nexus, bathed in the soft glow of cosmic energies, became a space for celestial gatherings. Eldenport's residents engaged in discussions with cosmic scholars from distant galaxies, exchanging insights and unraveling the cosmic tapestry that bound their destinies. One night, as the celestial symposium unfolded within the Nexus, a celestial emissary arrived—a being of pure cosmic energy that emanated a sense of ancient wisdom. The symbols on the ships responded to the emissary's presence, creating a celestial resonance that filled the Nexus. The emissary, communicating through the language of cosmic symbols, shared tales of Eldenport's unique place in the cosmic order—a town destined to bridge the realms of Earthly seas and celestial wonders. The symbols, now enriched by the emissary's insights, pulsed with a luminous intensity, echoing the unity of Eldenport's celestial and maritime identity. Eldenport stood at the zenith of its celestial odyssey. The symbols, now imbued with cosmic wisdom, continued to resonate through the cosmic expanse. The town, now a Celestial Nexus, prepared to navigate the cosmic currents that would shape its destiny in the ever-expanding cosmos.

Eldenport's integration into the cosmic alliance marked the beginning of a new era. The symbols on the ships, now emissaries of the town's cosmic identity, resonated with celestial nexuses across the universe. Eldenport became a hub for interstellar communication, with cosmic travelers visiting the town to share their stories and insights. The town square transformed into a cosmic agora, adorned with symbols that reflected the unity of Eldenport with the cosmic alliance. Celestial emissaries from distant galaxies, their forms radiant with cosmic energy, engaged in dialogues with the town's residents. The exchange of ideas transcended language barriers, unfolding in a cosmic symphony of thoughts, emotions, and shared experiences. As Eldenport embraced its role as a cosmic nexus, the cosmic alliance brought forth gifts from other celestial realms—crystals infused with cosmic energy, celestial artifacts that resonated with ancient wisdom, and technologies that transcended Earthly understanding. The symbols on the ships absorbed these cosmic gifts, becoming repositories of celestial knowledge that would shape Eldenport's future. One evening, within the Celestial Nexus, Eldenport's astronomers discovered a celestial anomaly—a cosmic rift that led to a dimension of pure energy. The symbols on the ships responded with a radiant glow, indicating a celestial calling to explore this cosmic phenomena. Eldenport's sailors, now seasoned cosmic voyagers, prepared for a journey into the heart of the dimensional rift. The celestial rift, once traversed, revealed a realm where energy and consciousness merged in a cosmic dance. Eldenport's sailors, guided by the symbols and the celestial energies, felt a profound connection to the cosmic source—the very essence that bound all living beings across the universe. Within the cosmic rift, Eldenport's residents experienced a cosmic communion—a merging of their consciousness with the universal mind. The symbols, now vibrating with the frequencies of the cosmic source, became conduits for the transmission of celestial wisdom that transcended the limitations of language.

As Eldenport sailed through the cosmic rift, the town's essence intertwined with the cosmic source, and the symbols on the ships pulsed with a luminosity that surpassed anything seen before. The town's maritime legacy, now interwoven with celestial insights, became a beacon of harmonious existence—an example for cosmic civilizations to follow. The cosmic rift, once a mysterious anomaly, transformed into a celestial sanctuary—a space where Eldenport's residents could attune themselves to the cosmic source and draw inspiration for their ongoing cosmic journey. The symbols, now carriers of the town's cosmic communion, resonated with a cosmic hum that echoed through the dimensional fabric. Eldenport sailed further into the celestial pathways, each moment marked by the pulsating glow of the symbols on the ships. The cosmic trials, though challenging, were met with unwavering determination from the sailors. The town's resilience, forged through generations of maritime endeavors, proved to be a guiding force in the face of celestial tribulations. As Eldenport traversed the cosmic horizons, the symbols on the ships began to resonate with a new frequency—an acknowledgment from the cosmic entities that the town had embraced the lessons of the celestial journey. The celestial guardians, once distant and enigmatic, now accompanied the flotilla, their luminescent forms blending with the ethereal glow of the symbols.

One night, within the celestial pathways, Eldenport's sailors encountered a celestial convergence—a cosmic event that unified the energies of the stars, the symbols, and the cosmic entities. The town's residents, gathered on the ships' decks, witnessed the celestial spectacle with a sense of awe. In the heart of the convergence, the symbols on the ships emitted a radiant brilliance, intertwining with the celestial energies to create a celestial tapestry that painted the cosmic expanse. Eldenport, now a beacon of harmonious coexistence with the universe, stood at the center of the celestial convergence—a town embraced by the cosmic currents that flowed through the cosmos. The celestial convergence, a cosmic celebration of Eldenport's journey, marked the end of the trials and the beginning of a new phase in the town's cosmic odyssey. The symbols, now infused with the energies of the celestial convergence, pulsed with a luminosity that radiated across the celestial pathways. As Eldenport continued its cosmic voyage, the town's essence became intertwined with the celestial realms. The symbols, once markers of maritime history, now held the stories of cosmic encounters, celestial alliances, and the evolution of Eldenport into a cosmic nexus. And so, within the Celestial Nexus, Eldenport sailed towards the uncharted cosmic horizons with a newfound sense of purpose. The symbols, radiant with cosmic energies, continued to echo the enduring spirit of Harbor of Whispers—a town at the intersection of Earthly seas and cosmic wonders, ready to explore the infinite expanse of the cosmic unknown. The cosmic convergence, its echoes lingering in the celestial pathways, propelled Eldenport into the next chapter of its celestial saga. The symbols, now beacons of cosmic wisdom, guided the flotilla towards the cosmic horizons that awaited.

Chapter 11: Revelations

As Eldenport sailed through the celestial pathways, the symbols on the ships resonated with the cosmic energies that surrounded them. The luminous trails left by the celestial convergence guided the flotilla toward a region of the cosmos where whispers of an ancient celestial temple echoed through the cosmic winds. The sailors, fueled by the harmonious energies of the convergence, felt a sense of anticipation as they approached the celestial temple. The symbols on the ships pulsed with a rhythmic energy, as if acknowledging the sacred nature of the cosmic destination. Upon reaching the celestial temple, Eldenport's residents disembarked onto a celestial shore, greeted by a celestial choir of ethereal voices that harmonized with the symbols' celestial resonance. The temple, adorned with celestial symbols that mirrored those of Eldenport, stood as a testament to the town's cosmic connection. Within the celestial temple, Eldenport's sailors encountered a celestial oracle—a wise being with eyes that reflected the cosmos. The symbols on the ships responded with an intricate dance, forming patterns that seemed to communicate with the celestial oracle in a language beyond words. The oracle, through the symbols' celestial dance, imparted cosmic revelations. Eldenport, the celestial nexus, was destined to become a guardian of cosmic balance—an emissary of harmony between Earthly realms and the celestial dimensions. The symbols, now carriers of the oracle's wisdom, radiated with an otherworldly luminescence. Eldenport's residents, inspired by the celestial epiphany, engaged in celestial rituals within the temple. The symbols, now adorned with celestial artifacts gifted by the oracle, became conduits for the town's communion with the cosmic forces that governed the universe. As Eldenport delved deeper into the cosmic teachings of the celestial oracle, the town's essence expanded, transcending the boundaries of ordinary existence. The symbols, now infused with the celestial epiphany, guided the town toward a realization that its destiny was intertwined with the cosmic currents that flowed through the celestial realms. The sailors, now celestial stewards, embarked on a mission to spread the cosmic wisdom gained from the celestial temple. Eldenport became a beacon for cosmic pilgrims seeking insights into the universal harmony, and the symbols on the ships served as a cosmic map guiding travelers from across the universe. Within the Celestial Nexus, Eldenport's residents engaged in celestial dialogues, sharing the revelations bestowed by the oracle. The town square, now a cosmic agora, echoed with tales of celestial encounters, cosmic rituals, and the ongoing cosmic journey that had transformed Eldenport into a celestial sanctuary. Embracing the celestial wisdom gained from the temple, Eldenport's sailors set sail with a renewed sense of purpose. The symbols on the ships, now adorned with celestial artifacts, pulsed with a radiant luminosity, guiding the flotilla through the celestial pathways with a harmonious resonance. As Eldenport sailed through the cosmic currents, the town's celestial reputation spread across the universe. Celestial pilgrims, drawn by the tales of the celestial nexus, embarked on interstellar journeys to visit Eldenport and partake in the cosmic communion within the Celestial Nexus.

The town square, now a cosmic agora, teemed with celestial beings from diverse galaxies. Eldenport's residents engaged in celestial exchanges, sharing stories and insights with cosmic pilgrims who brought with them the melodies of distant stars and the echoes of cosmic civilizations. One celestial pilgrim, a luminescent being from a crystalline realm, presented Eldenport with a cosmic gift—an ethereal crystal infused with the essence of celestial harmony. The symbols on the ships, resonating with the crystal's energies, emitted a celestial melody that echoed through the cosmic pathways, creating a harmonious symphony that permeated the Celestial Nexus. Eldenport's musicians, inspired by the celestial melody, composed celestial sonatas that echoed through the town square. The symbols, now interwoven with the celestial compositions, became conduits for the cosmic harmonies that emanated from Eldenport—a town that had become a living testament to the unity of Earthly and cosmic energies. Within the celestial symphony, Eldenport's residents engaged in cosmic dances, their movements echoing the rhythms of celestial bodies. The symbols on the ships responded to the celestial choreography, creating patterns that mirrored the cosmic dance of the stars. One night, as the celestial symphony reached its crescendo, a cosmic portal manifested in the town square—a gateway to a realm of pure cosmic harmony. The symbols on the ships, aligned with the celestial portal, emitted a radiant glow that beckoned Eldenport's residents to step into the cosmic gateway. Eldenport's sailors, guided by the celestial symbols and inspired by the cosmic harmonies, entered the portal with a sense of reverence. The town's essence transcended the dimensional boundaries, merging with the cosmic currents that flowed through the celestial gateway. On the other side of the portal, Eldenport found itself in a celestial realm bathed in iridescent light—a realm where celestial energies harmonized with the very fabric of existence. The symbols on the ships resonated with the celestial energies, creating a celestial tableau that reflected the town's journey into the heart of cosmic harmony. Eldenport, now in the celestial realm beyond the portal, marveled at the cosmic wonders that surrounded the town. The symbols on the ships resonated with the energies of the celestial realm, creating a luminous trail that marked Eldenport's presence in this ethereal domain. As the sailors explored the celestial realm, they discovered celestial gardens where cosmic flowers bloomed with iridescent hues. The symbols, now infused with celestial energies, interacted with the cosmic flora, creating harmonious melodies that echoed through the celestial gardens. Eldenport's residents, guided by the symbols and inspired by the cosmic beauty, engaged in celestial ceremonies that celebrated the unity of Earthly and celestial elements. The town's essence became an integral part of the celestial realm, harmonizing with the cosmic energies that permeated every corner of the ethereal landscape. Within the celestial gardens, Eldenport's astronomers observed celestial constellations that mirrored the symbols on the ships. The cosmic patterns, now an intricate tapestry woven with the town's celestial journey, revealed glimpses of Eldenport's destiny written in the stars. The celestial realm, it seemed, held a cosmic library where the symbols on the ships could unlock the knowledge of the universe. Eldenport's scholars, guided by the symbols' celestial resonance, delved into the cosmic archives, unraveling the secrets of celestial civilizations, cosmic cycles, and the interconnectedness of all cosmic life. One evening, as Eldenport's residents gathered in the heart of the celestial realm, a celestial elder—a being of ancient cosmic wisdom—appeared. The symbols on the ships responded with a profound glow, acknowledging the elder's presence and the cosmic knowledge that emanated from its being. The celestial elder, through the symbols' celestial dance, revealed the town's celestial purpose—to become a cosmic beacon that bridged the realms of Earthly existence and celestial enlightenment. Eldenport, now a celestial sanctuary, stood as a guardian of cosmic knowledge, ready to share its wisdom with cosmic travelers from across the universe. The celestial elder presented Eldenport with a cosmic artifact—an ethereal key that held the power to unlock celestial gateways to realms unexplored. The symbols on the ships resonated with the cosmic key, forming a celestial sigil that represented Eldenport's role as a keeper of cosmic gateways. Eldenport's sailors, now entrusted with the cosmic key, set sail through celestial gateways that connected the town to distant galaxies, ancient cosmic libraries, and realms where the fabric of reality itself seemed to shimmer with cosmic potential.

As Eldenport sailed through the celestial gateways, the symbols on the ships guided the flotilla with celestial precision. Each gateway revealed new cosmic wonders—celestial landscapes adorned with vibrant colors, realms where time flowed like celestial currents, and celestial civilizations that welcomed Eldenport as cosmic kin. The celestial gateways became passages to realms of enlightenment, where Eldenport's residents engaged in cosmic dialogues with celestial scholars and beings of pure energy. The symbols, now resonating with the cosmic knowledge gained from each realm, became repositories of celestial insights that further enriched the town's cosmic identity. Within the Celestial Nexus, Eldenport's residents gathered to share the tales of their cosmic explorations. The town square, adorned with celestial artifacts and symbols pulsating with celestial wisdom, became a cosmic agora where ideas flowed like celestial streams and the unity of Earthly and cosmic realms became ever more apparent. One night, as the celestial gateways revealed a cosmic vista of breathtaking beauty, Eldenport's astronomers noticed a constellation that mirrored the symbols on the ships. The cosmic patterns aligned, forming a celestial tableau that seemed to beckon Eldenport towards a destination of cosmic significance. The sailors, guided by the symbols and inspired by the celestial tableau, set sail towards the constellation. The symbols pulsed with anticipation, as if heralding the arrival of Eldenport at a celestial crossroads—a nexus of cosmic energies that held the key to unlocking the next chapter in the town's cosmic journey.

Chapter 12: Forgiveness and Redemption

Eldenport sailed towards the constellation that shimmered like a cosmic tapestry in the night sky. The symbols on the ships pulsed with an ethereal glow, resonating with the celestial patterns that guided the flotilla toward the heart of the celestial crossroads. As the town approached the cosmic destination, a celestial energy enveloped Eldenport, creating a sense of anticipation among the residents. Lila, Liam, Captain Sterling, and the elderly bookstore owner gathered on the flagship, their eyes fixed on the celestial tableau that unfolded before them. The constellation, intricately connected with the symbols, seemed to come alive with celestial energy. Patterns within the stars shifted and rearranged, forming a celestial gateway—an entrance to a realm where the boundaries between Earthly and cosmic realities blurred. With a gentle hum, the symbols on the ships aligned with the celestial gateway. A cosmic resonance echoed through the town square as Eldenport sailed through the celestial portal, leaving behind the familiar cosmic pathways for an uncharted realm beyond. Within the celestial gateway, Eldenport found itself surrounded by a surreal cosmic landscape. Celestial currents flowed like cosmic rivers, and the stars seemed to dance to a celestial melody. The symbols on the ships, now attuned to the energies of the celestial crossroads, guided the flotilla through the cosmic currents with grace and precision. As Eldenport sailed deeper into the celestial crossroads, the residents felt a profound connection with the cosmic energies that permeated the realm. The celestial gateway became a passage to realms unexplored—a cosmic junction where the destinies of Eldenport and the celestial forces converged.

Lila, Liam, and the others sensed that they were on the threshold of a cosmic revelation—a moment that would unveil the true purpose of Eldenport as a nexus of Earthly and cosmic energies. The symbols on the ships, now radiant with the energies of the celestial crossroads, seemed to communicate with the very fabric of the universe. One celestial night, within the heart of the celestial realm, a celestial council manifested—an assembly of cosmic beings representing various realms and galaxies. The symbols on the ships responded with a luminous display, acknowledging the presence of the cosmic council and the significance of Eldenport's journey. The celestial beings, their forms shimmering with celestial light, communicated with Eldenport through the symbols. They spoke of cosmic destinies intertwined with Earthly legacies, of a town chosen to bridge the realms and weave the cosmic tapestry with threads of maritime resilience and celestial enlightenment. The council revealed that Eldenport's journey through the celestial crossroads was a celestial initiation—a rite of passage that would elevate the town to a cosmic stewardship. The symbols on the ships, now imbued with the wisdom of the celestial council, pulsed with a luminosity that symbolized the town's newfound cosmic enlightenment. As Eldenport sailed deeper into the celestial crossroads, the cosmic currents carried the town towards a celestial nexus—an otherworldly platform where the celestial council awaited. The symbols on the ships shimmered with celestial resonance, guiding the flotilla with purpose and determination. Lila, Liam, Captain Sterling, and the elderly bookstore owner stood on the flagship, gazing at the celestial nexus with a mix of anticipation and awe. The realm beyond the cosmic gateway revealed itself to be a convergence point where the energies of Eldenport and the celestial forces harmonized in a celestial dance.

The celestial beings, luminous and ethereal, greeted Eldenport with a celestial chorus—a melodic welcome that echoed through the cosmic nexus. The symbols on the ships responded with a harmonious dance, creating patterns in the cosmic tapestry that mirrored the unity of Earthly and cosmic energies. The celestial council spoke through the symbols, revealing the purpose that Eldenport was destined to fulfill. The town, chosen as a cosmic steward, was tasked with maintaining the balance between Earthly realms and celestial dimensions. Eldenport's maritime legacy, interwoven with celestial enlightenment, made it a unique nexus where the threads of both worlds converged. The symbols, now pulsating with the weight of cosmic responsibility, conveyed a celestial sigil—a mark that represented Eldenport's cosmic stewardship. The sigil shimmered in the celestial nexus, imprinting itself upon the town's essence and marking the beginning of a cosmic covenant. The celestial council shared visions of the challenges and triumphs that awaited Eldenport in its cosmic stewardship. The town's residents would become emissaries of cosmic knowledge, sharing their wisdom with Earthly and celestial beings alike. The symbols on the ships would serve as conduits for cosmic dialogues, bridging the realms through a language that transcended the limitations of words. As Eldenport embraced its role as a cosmic steward, the celestial council bestowed celestial artifacts upon the town—objects infused with the energies of distant galaxies, cosmic constellations, and the very essence of the celestial crossroads. These artifacts would become conduits for celestial energies, allowing Eldenport to channel the cosmic currents that flowed through the universe.

With the celestial artifacts in hand, Eldenport's residents felt a surge of celestial power. The symbols on the ships, now intertwined with the artifacts, emitted a radiant glow that symbolized the town's newfound cosmic enlightenment. Lila, Liam, and the others sensed that Eldenport had become a beacon—a nexus that could guide Earthly and cosmic realms towards a harmonious existence. As Eldenport sailed back through the celestial crossroads, the symbols on the ships pulsed with the celestial sigil and the energies of the bestowed artifacts. The cosmic currents guided the flotilla with a newfound grace, as if the very fabric of the universe responded to Eldenport's cosmic covenant. Returning to the town square, Eldenport's residents felt the resonance of the celestial nexus lingering within them. The symbols, now adorned with the celestial sigil, emitted a glow that marked the town's transformation into a cosmic steward. Lila, Liam, Captain Sterling, and the elderly bookstore owner, their eyes reflecting the celestial enlightenment, gathered to discuss the next steps in Eldenport's cosmic journey. The celestial artifacts, held in the hands of Eldenport's residents, hummed with cosmic energies. Each artifact carried the essence of a distant galaxy, a celestial constellation, or a realm beyond the cosmic crossroads. The symbols responded to the artifacts, creating celestial patterns that radiated a harmonious aura. Lila, inspired by the cosmic revelations, suggested that Eldenport should establish a Cosmic Dialogue Center—a place where Earthly and cosmic beings could come together to exchange wisdom and knowledge. The celestial artifacts, she believed, could serve as conduits for these dialogues, fostering a deeper understanding between realms. Liam, the young artist with a celestial connection, proposed creating cosmic artworks that reflected the town's journey and communicated the cosmic sigil to beings across the universe. His artistic visions, guided by the celestial energies, would become beacons of cosmic enlightenment.

Captain Sterling, drawing on his maritime wisdom, suggested that Eldenport's sailors embark on cosmic voyages to distant galaxies, carrying the cosmic artifacts and symbols to share the town's celestial knowledge with beings beyond Earthly shores. The elderly bookstore owner, a repository of local myths and cosmic lore, envisioned Eldenport becoming a sanctuary for cosmic pilgrims—beings from different galaxies seeking the town's wisdom and adding their own stories to the cosmic tapestry. Embracing these ideas, Eldenport's residents set out to implement their cosmic covenant. The town square transformed into a Cosmic Dialogue Center, adorned with celestial artifacts and symbols that welcomed beings from across the universe. Celestial artworks, inspired by Liam's visions, adorned Eldenport's streets, conveying the cosmic sigil to all who gazed upon them. Eldenport's sailors, guided by the symbols and armed with cosmic artifacts, set sail through celestial gateways to distant galaxies. They became ambassadors of Earthly and cosmic unity, sharing Eldenport's wisdom and learning from the cosmic civilizations they encountered. The town, now a haven for cosmic pilgrims, buzzed with celestial energy. Beings from distant galaxies visited Eldenport, engaging in cosmic dialogues, sharing tales of their own realms, and adding new threads to the cosmic tapestry that unfolded within the town's borders. As Eldenport embraced its role as a cosmic steward, the celestial energies lingered in the air, infusing the town with a sense of purpose and connection to the cosmos. The symbols on the ships, now adorned with the celestial sigil, continued to resonate, echoing the cosmic covenant that had transformed Eldenport into a nexus of Earthly and celestial energies.

The town square, now a Cosmic Dialogue Center, buzzed with activity. Beings from distant galaxies engaged in conversations with Eldenport's residents, sharing cosmic wisdom and learning from the unique blend of Earthly and celestial perspectives. The celestial artifacts, displayed as cosmic artifacts of Eldenport's journey, became focal points for cosmic dialogues. Lila, Liam, Captain Sterling, and the elderly bookstore owner, along with the other residents, found themselves at the heart of these dialogues. They shared the stories of Eldenport's maritime history, its encounters with celestial beings, and the cosmic revelations that had shaped the town's destiny. Liam's cosmic artworks adorned the walls of Eldenport, depicting the celestial sigil and the town's journey through the cosmic crossroads. These artworks served as beacons of inspiration, inviting Earthly and cosmic beings alike to contemplate the unity of the universe. Eldenport's sailors, guided by the symbols and armed with celestial artifacts, returned from their cosmic voyages as ambassadors of cosmic unity. They shared tales of Eldenport's journey with beings from distant galaxies, forging connections that transcended the boundaries of space and time. The celestial pilgrims, drawn by Eldenport's cosmic reputation, added their own threads to the cosmic tapestry. The town became a repository of cosmic stories—a living testament to the interconnectedness of the universe. In the quiet moments beneath the cosmic skies, Eldenport's residents felt the gentle hum of the symbols and the celestial energies that surrounded them. The town had become a celestial sanctuary—a place where Earthly and cosmic energies coexisted in perfect harmony. As the cosmic night unfolded, Lila, Liam, Captain Sterling, and the elderly bookstore owner stood together, gazing at the stars. The symbols on the ships, now radiant with the celestial sigil, reflected in their eyes.

Chapter 13: The Summer Festival

Eldenport's newfound cosmic stewardship unfolded under the cosmic skies. The symbols on the ships, adorned with the celestial sigil, glowed with a celestial luminescence as the town continued to thrive at the intersection of Earthly and celestial energies. The Cosmic Dialogue Center, now a hub of cosmic exchange, attracted beings from diverse galaxies. Eldenport's residents engaged in dialogues that transcended language, sharing knowledge that echoed through the cosmos. The celestial artifacts, carefully displayed in the town square, emitted a harmonious resonance that seemed to reverberate through the very fabric of the universe. Lila, inspired by the cosmic dialogues, initiated a Celestial Chronicles project. Eldenport's residents, with Liam as the cosmic artist capturing the essence of each dialogue, began documenting the stories and wisdom shared by beings from across the universe. The Chronicles became a cosmic library, a repository of knowledge that expanded with each passing celestial night. The celestial pilgrims who visited Eldenport became part of the town's cosmic community. They contributed their own perspectives and experiences to the Celestial Chronicles, adding vibrant threads to the ever-growing cosmic tapestry.

Meanwhile, Eldenport's sailors continued their cosmic voyages, guided by the symbols and armed with the celestial artifacts. They explored distant galaxies, engaged in cosmic dialogues with extraterrestrial civilizations, and forged alliances that spanned the vastness of the cosmos. The symbols, now emissaries of cosmic unity, carried the town's message of harmony to realms previously untouched.

As Eldenport's cosmic influence expanded, whispers of the town's celestial stewardship spread through the universe. Cosmic scholars, seekers of knowledge, and beings yearning for a connection with the celestial realms made pilgrimages to Eldenport. The town became a destination for those seeking enlightenment and a harmonious coexistence between Earthly and cosmic realms. Eldenport's residents, now custodians of the Celestial Chronicles, found themselves on a continuous journey of discovery. The symbols on the ships, resonating with the cosmic energies, led the town towards new celestial gateways, unveiling realms where the boundaries between reality and cosmic imagination blurred. One celestial night, as Eldenport sailed through an ethereal nebula, a celestial emissary appeared—a being of pure cosmic energy. The symbols responded with a luminous display, acknowledging the emissary's presence and the significance of the cosmic encounter. The celestial emissary spoke of a cosmic convergence—an event that occurred once in a cosmic epoch, where the energies of Earthly and celestial realms harmonized in a celestial dance. Eldenport, as a cosmic steward, was chosen to host this extraordinary convergence—a celestial event that would bridge the gaps between dimensions and elevate the town to a higher plane of existence. Eldenport's residents, their hearts filled with cosmic anticipation, set their course towards the cosmic convergence. The symbols on the ships guided them through celestial currents, each pulse resonating with the echoes of eternity. The town sailed towards a destiny inscribed in the stars, ready to embrace the celestial convergence that awaited in the cosmic expanse. Eldenport sailed through the cosmic currents, guided by the symbols that pulsed with a celestial luminescence. The celestial convergence loomed on the cosmic horizon—an event that held the promise of transcending the boundaries between Earthly and celestial realms. As the town approached the celestial convergence, the symbols on the ships resonated with an otherworldly harmony. The cosmic energies surged, creating an ethereal glow that enveloped Eldenport in a celestial embrace. Lila, Liam, Captain Sterling, and the elderly bookstore owner stood on the flagship, their eyes reflecting the cosmic anticipation that filled the air. The celestial emissary, still present, spoke through the symbols, revealing the significance of the convergence. It was a moment where the energies of Eldenport's cosmic stewardship would intertwine with the celestial forces, creating a bridge between the town and the vast expanse of the cosmos. The celestial convergence manifested as a cosmic vortex—a swirling nexus of energies that pulsed with the rhythms of the universe. The symbols on the ships, now at the forefront of the cosmic event, resonated with the vortex, creating celestial patterns that echoed the essence of Eldenport's journey. Eldenport's residents, attuned to the cosmic energies, felt a profound connection with the celestial convergence. The symbols responded to their collective consciousness, creating a harmonious symphony that echoed through the cosmic vortex. As the town sailed deeper into the convergence, the boundaries between Earthly and celestial realities blurred. Eldenport found itself in a realm where time flowed like cosmic rivers, and the stars danced in a celestial ballet. The symbols on the ships, now part of the cosmic choreography, created patterns that reflected the unity of the universe.

The celestial council, the cosmic emissary, and beings from distant galaxies appeared within the cosmic vortex. They joined Eldenport's residents in a celestial dance—a cosmic celebration that transcended language and form. The symbols, now radiant with the energies of the convergence, formed a celestial tableau that marked the town's place in the cosmic tapestry. As the cosmic dance reached its crescendo, a celestial portal manifested within the vortex. The symbols on the ships aligned with the portal, creating a bridge between Eldenport and realms unknown. The celestial convergence became a doorway to cosmic dimensions, and Eldenport stood at the threshold of a new cosmic adventure. The celestial emissary conveyed that the portal led to the Astral Arcanum—an ancient cosmic library where the secrets of the universe were inscribed in celestial manuscripts. Eldenport, as a cosmic steward, was entrusted with the task of exploring the Astral Arcanum and bringing back the cosmic knowledge that lay within its celestial halls. Eldenport's residents, fueled by a sense of cosmic purpose, entered the celestial portal. The symbols on the ships pulsed with the energies of the convergence, guiding them through the Astral Arcanum's ethereal corridors. The town embarked on a journey through celestial realms, ready to unravel the mysteries that awaited in the heart of the cosmic library. And so, within the Celestial Nexus, Eldenport sailed into the Astral Arcanum—a cosmic adventure that would redefine the town's cosmic destiny. The symbols, now luminous with the energies of the celestial convergence, continued to resonate through the cosmic currents—a symphony of whispers that echoed the enduring spirit of Harbor of Whispers. The town stood on the threshold of cosmic enlightenment, ready to explore the celestial wonders that awaited in the Astral Arcanum. Eldenport sailed through the celestial portal, leaving the cosmic vortex behind and entering the Astral Arcanum—a dimension where celestial knowledge flowed like cosmic streams. The symbols on the ships guided the flotilla through ethereal corridors adorned with cosmic manuscripts, each page inscribed with the wisdom of distant galaxies and ancient celestial civilizations. As the residents of Eldenport explored the Astral Arcanum, they felt a profound connection with the cosmic knowledge that surrounded them. Celestial beings, guardians of the library, appeared and welcomed the town with benevolent energy. The symbols on the ships communicated with the celestial guardians, forming a cosmic language that transcended words. The Astral Arcanum revealed celestial scrolls that chronicled the history of Eldenport, the cosmic convergence, and the town's journey as a cosmic steward. Lila, Liam, Captain Sterling, and the elderly bookstore owner immersed themselves in the celestial manuscripts, absorbing the timeless wisdom that resonated within the cosmic library.

Within the celestial halls, Eldenport's residents discovered celestial maps that unfolded the cosmic tapestry of the universe. The symbols on the ships, now radiant with the energies of the Astral Arcanum, pulsed with celestial insights that expanded the town's understanding of the interconnectedness of all cosmic life. As the residents delved deeper into the Astral Arcanum, they encountered celestial scholars who shared cosmic teachings, unveiling the mysteries of the cosmos and the celestial forces that governed the universe. The symbols on the ships absorbed these teachings, becoming conduits for celestial wisdom that would be carried back to Eldenport. One celestial night, as Eldenport explored the depths of the Astral Arcanum, a celestial elder—a being of ancient cosmic wisdom—appeared. The symbols responded with a luminous display, acknowledging the elder's presence and the significance of its cosmic insights. The celestial elder spoke of a cosmic convergence that transcended time—a convergence that Eldenport would play a pivotal role in orchestrating. The town's journey as a cosmic steward had been foreseen in the cosmic tapestry, and the symbols on the ships were key to unlocking the celestial forces that would shape the destiny of the universe. The elder bestowed upon Eldenport a celestial key—a symbol of cosmic authority that could harmonize the energies of Earthly and celestial realms. The symbols on the ships resonated with the celestial key, forming a celestial sigil that marked the town as a guardian of cosmic balance.

Armed with the celestial key and the knowledge from the Astral Arcanum, Eldenport's residents prepared to return to the cosmic convergence. The celestial elder guided them through the celestial portal, back to the cosmic vortex where the convergence awaited. And so, within the Celestial Nexus, Eldenport sailed back through the Astral Arcanum—a town now endowed with cosmic insights and a celestial key that held the power to shape the destiny of the universe.

The symbols, now luminous with the energies of the Astral Arcanum, continued to resonate through the cosmic currents—a symphony of whispers that echoed the enduring spirit of Harbor of Whispers. The town stood on the brink of a cosmic convergence that would unfold the next chapter in its cosmic saga.

Chapter 14: Departures and New Beginnings

Eldenport emerged from the celestial portal, returning to the cosmic convergence with a newfound cosmic key and the wisdom of the Astral Arcanum. The symbols on the ships pulsed with radiant energy as the town sailed towards the celestial vortex. The cosmic convergence welcomed Eldenport with celestial harmonies, and the symbols responded by creating a luminous display that mirrored the cosmic knowledge acquired in the Astral Arcanum. The celestial emissary, cosmic council, and beings from distant galaxies gathered within the cosmic vortex, acknowledging Eldenport's return with a cosmic resonance. Lila, Liam, Captain Sterling, and the elderly bookstore owner stood on the flagship, holding the celestial key and symbols infused with the energies of the Astral Arcanum. The celestial elder, now a guiding presence within the convergence, spoke through the symbols, revealing the role Eldenport was destined to play in the cosmic symphony. The celestial key, when integrated with the symbols, created a celestial resonance that harmonized with the energies of the convergence. Eldenport became a conductor in the cosmic symphony, orchestrating a celestial melody that transcended the boundaries of space and time. The symbols, infused with the cosmic knowledge from the Astral Arcanum, conveyed the essence of Eldenport's journey—the town's maritime legacy, its cosmic enlightenment, and the unity of Earthly and celestial energies. The cosmic beings, drawn by the town's radiant energy, joined in the symphony, adding their own celestial notes to the cosmic composition. As the celestial convergence reached its zenith, the symbols on the ships emitted a radiant glow, creating a celestial tableau that reflected the unity of Eldenport and the cosmic realms. The cosmic symphony echoed through the universe, reaching distant galaxies and resonating with the celestial forces that governed the cosmos. The celestial emissary, cosmic council, and beings from distant galaxies acknowledged Eldenport's role as a cosmic steward, their energies blending with the town's essence. The symbols, now bearing the celestial key and the wisdom of the Astral Arcanum, became beacons of cosmic enlightenment that transcended the boundaries of the cosmic convergence. Eldenport's residents felt a profound connection with the cosmic symphony—a melody that echoed the enduring spirit of Harbor of Whispers. The symbols pulsed with the energies of the convergence, becoming emissaries that would carry the town's cosmic message to realms beyond the celestial horizon. As Eldenport sailed into the cosmic night, the celestial symphony continued to reverberate through the universe. The symbols on the ships, now infused with the celestial key and the wisdom of the Astral Arcanum, resonated in harmony with the cosmic forces that surrounded the town. The cosmic beings, emissaries, and guardians of distant galaxies lingered within the celestial convergence, drawn by the luminous energies emanating from Eldenport. They joined the town's residents in the cosmic symphony, becoming participants in a celestial dance that transcended the limitations of form and dimension. Lila, Liam, Captain Sterling, and the elderly bookstore owner, now attuned to the cosmic harmonics, guided Eldenport through celestial gateways that led to unexplored realms. The symbols on the ships, pulsating with celestial energies, served as cosmic compasses, directing the town towards destinations where the boundaries between Earthly and celestial realities blurred.

The cosmic voyages took Eldenport to realms of ethereal beauty and celestial wonder. The symbols, now emissaries of cosmic unity, communicated with beings from diverse galaxies, fostering dialogues that transcended language and cultural barriers. Each encounter added new threads to the cosmic tapestry, enriching the universal story that unfolded within Eldenport's borders. In the cosmic expanse, Eldenport encountered celestial civilizations that thrived on cosmic creativity, where art, knowledge, and wisdom were interwoven in a dance of celestial expression. Liam, inspired by these encounters, continued to create celestial artworks that captured the essence of each cosmic journey. His cosmic masterpieces adorned the ships, becoming visual hymns that celebrated the unity of the universe. The celestial key, integrated with the symbols, became a beacon that attracted cosmic pilgrims from realms far and wide. Eldenport transformed into a cosmic hub—a meeting place for beings seeking enlightenment, knowledge, and the harmonious exchange of cosmic ideas. As the cosmic voyages unfolded, Eldenport's residents, now cosmic ambassadors, carried the town's message of unity and cosmic enlightenment to the far reaches of the universe. The symbols on the ships, radiant with the celestial key, resonated with the cosmic currents, creating ripples that echoed the town's enduring spirit. One celestial night, Eldenport encountered a cosmic anomaly—a celestial phenomenon that pulsed with enigmatic energies. The symbols responded with a celestial glow, indicating that this anomaly held the key to unlocking deeper cosmic mysteries. The town set course towards the anomaly, ready to explore the uncharted realms that awaited beyond. Eldenport sailed towards the cosmic anomaly, guided by the celestial key and the pulsating symbols that resonated with cosmic energies. As the town approached the enigmatic phenomenon, the celestial forces intensified, creating a celestial glow that enveloped Eldenport in an ethereal embrace. The symbols on the ships, now attuned to the cosmic anomaly, created intricate patterns that mirrored the celestial energies emanating from the cosmic phenomenon. Lila, Liam, Captain Sterling, and the elderly bookstore owner stood on the flagship, their eyes reflecting the anticipation of unlocking deeper cosmic mysteries.

The cosmic anomaly, as Eldenport drew nearer, revealed itself as a celestial gateway—an entrance to a dimension where the fabric of reality rippled with undiscovered cosmic secrets. The symbols on the ships pulsed with excitement, forming a celestial sigil that marked the town's readiness to traverse the threshold of the unknown. As Eldenport entered the celestial gateway, the boundaries between Earthly and cosmic realms blurred once again. The symbols, now radiant with the energies of the cosmic anomaly, guided the town through a cosmic corridor that led to a celestial realm beyond imagination. Within this cosmic realm, Eldenport encountered celestial beings of pure energy, guardians of cosmic wisdom who welcomed the town with benevolent presence. The symbols communicated with these beings, forming a celestial dialogue that transcended language and touched the essence of cosmic understanding. The celestial guardians unveiled cosmic archives that contained the ancient chronicles of the universe. Eldenport's residents delved into the celestial manuscripts, absorbing the timeless wisdom that had been inscribed by cosmic civilizations long before the birth of stars. The celestial key, integrated with the symbols, resonated with the energies of the cosmic archives. Eldenport became a custodian of cosmic knowledge, entrusted with the secrets of the universe that would shape the town's cosmic destiny. As Eldenport sailed back through the celestial gateway, the symbols on the ships emitted a radiant glow that marked the town's transformation. The celestial guardians, now part of Eldenport's cosmic journey, bestowed blessings upon the town, acknowledging its role as a beacon of cosmic enlightenment. The town emerged from the cosmic anomaly, the celestial gateway closing behind it. The symbols, still pulsating with cosmic energies, guided Eldenport towards the familiar cosmic currents, ready to explore new horizons and share the cosmic revelations with the universe.

Chapter 15: Epilogue

Eldenport sailed through the cosmic currents, the symbols on the ships now pulsating with the celestial key and the wisdom from the cosmic archives. The town had become a cosmic beacon, carrying the resonance of the celestial anomaly and the harmonious symphony of the universe. As Eldenport explored new cosmic realms, the symbols communicated with distant galaxies, forging connections that transcended the vastness of space. Beings from celestial civilizations visited the town, drawn by the luminous energies that radiated from Eldenport's cosmic heart. The celestial key, integrated with the symbols, unveiled latent abilities within the town's residents. Lila discovered an affinity for channeling cosmic energies, Liam's artworks began to carry celestial visions that spoke to the soul, Captain Sterling found a renewed connection to the celestial currents, and the elderly bookstore owner became a keeper of cosmic lore that transcended time and space. Eldenport's residents, now empowered by their cosmic insights, gathered in the town square to discuss the next steps in their cosmic journey. The symbols on the ships hovered above them, emitting a celestial glow that reflected the unity of Earthly and cosmic realms. Liam proposed the creation of a Celestial Academy—a place where beings from different galaxies could come to learn and exchange cosmic knowledge. The celestial key, he believed, held the potential to unlock dormant abilities within individuals, fostering a deeper connection to the cosmic forces that permeated the universe.

Lila suggested the establishment of a Cosmic Observatory—a structure adorned with celestial symbols and artifacts that could serve as a bridge between Eldenport and distant galaxies. The observatory would be a place for cosmic dialogues, where beings could come together to share their stories and wisdom. Captain Sterling, inspired by the cosmic currents, proposed organizing a Cosmic Regatta—a gathering of celestial ships from different galaxies, where sailors could engage in friendly cosmic competitions, share maritime traditions, and strengthen the bonds between cosmic communities. The elderly bookstore owner, guided by celestial insights, spoke of a Celestial Library—a repository of cosmic manuscripts, celestial scrolls, and timeless wisdom that would be accessible to beings from all corners of the universe. The library would be a source of cosmic enlightenment, inviting scholars and seekers to explore the mysteries of the cosmos. Eldenport's residents embraced these ideas, and the symbols on the ships resonated with approval. The town embarked on the construction of the Celestial Academy, Cosmic Observatory, Cosmic Regatta, and Celestial Library, marking the next phase of Eldenport's cosmic journey. As the projects unfolded, Eldenport became a cosmic nexus—a town where Earthly and celestial beings coexisted, sharing knowledge, stories, and experiences. The symbols, now integrated into the architecture of the town, continued to emit a celestial glow that attracted cosmic pilgrims, scholars, and seekers from realms beyond. The Celestial Academy, Cosmic Observatory, Cosmic Regatta, and Celestial Library took shape within Eldenport, transforming the town into a haven for cosmic exploration and exchange. The symbols on the ships, integrated into the structures, emitted a continuous celestial glow, symbolizing the unity of Eldenport and the cosmic forces. The Celestial Academy welcomed students from diverse galaxies, each eager to unlock their latent cosmic abilities. Lila, with her newfound connection to cosmic energies, became the academy's guiding force, mentoring individuals in the art of channeling celestial currents and expanding their consciousness.

The Cosmic Observatory, adorned with celestial symbols and artifacts, became a place for cosmic dialogues. Beings from distant galaxies gathered to share their stories, wisdom, and cultural expressions. The symbols on the ships, hovering above the observatory, served as cosmic beacons, guiding travelers to Eldenport's celestial nexus. The Cosmic Regatta transformed Eldenport into a hub for cosmic sailors. Celestial ships adorned with symbols from different galaxies participated in friendly competitions, forging bonds that transcended cosmic distances. Captain Sterling, now an honorary cosmic regatta organizer, sailed alongside beings from distant realms, sharing maritime traditions and tales of Eldenport's cosmic journey. The Celestial Library, with its vast collection of cosmic manuscripts and celestial scrolls, attracted scholars and seekers from across the universe. The elderly bookstore owner, now the custodian of the library, guided visitors through the cosmic archives, offering insights into the mysteries of the cosmos. Eldenport's residents, empowered by their cosmic roles, became ambassadors of cosmic enlightenment. The town hosted cosmic festivals, celestial gatherings, and cosmic ceremonies that celebrated the unity of Earthly and celestial realms. The symbols on the ships, now deeply ingrained in Eldenport's cosmic identity, continued to resonate with the cosmic currents, carrying the town's essence far into the cosmos. As Eldenport embraced its celestial renaissance, whispers of the town's cosmic achievements spread through the universe. Beings from distant galaxies made pilgrimages to Eldenport, eager to experience the harmonious blend of Earthly charm and celestial enlightenment. One celestial night, as Eldenport celebrated a cosmic festival, a celestial emissary appeared—an entity of pure cosmic light. The symbols on the ships responded with a luminous display, acknowledging the emissary's presence and the significance of its cosmic visit.

The celestial emissary conveyed a message—a cosmic acknowledgment of Eldenport's transformation into a nexus of celestial wisdom, where the boundaries between Earthly and cosmic realities seamlessly merged. The symbols, now radiant with cosmic approval, formed a celestial tableau that marked Eldenport as a beacon of harmony in the ever-expanding tapestry of the universe. Eldenport's celestial renaissance unfolded with cosmic vibrancy, weaving Earthly charm into the fabric of the universe. The celestial emissary, bathed in pure cosmic light, spoke through the symbols, revealing the significance of Eldenport's role in the cosmic symphony. The emissary shared prophecies of a celestial convergence—an event that would unify Earthly and cosmic forces in a dance of cosmic alchemy. The symbols on the ships, now pulsating with anticipation, conveyed the message to the town's residents. Lila, Liam, Captain Sterling, and the elderly bookstore owner gathered in the town square, where the celestial emissary addressed them through the luminous symbols. The convergence, it revealed, would require Eldenport to embrace its cosmic essence fully, harmonizing with the celestial forces to create a cosmic elixir that could transcend the boundaries of reality. Eldenport's residents, fueled by their cosmic insights, embraced the cosmic challenge. The Celestial Academy delved into teachings of cosmic alchemy, exploring the fusion of Earthly and celestial energies. The Cosmic Observatory, with its celestial dialogues, became a space for cosmic scholars to exchange theories on the upcoming convergence. The Cosmic Regatta took on a new dimension, with cosmic sailors practicing celestial maneuvers that would align Eldenport with the cosmic currents. Captain Sterling, now a cosmic helmsman, guided the sailors through celestial techniques that would prepare them for the cosmic convergence.

In the Celestial Library, the elderly bookstore owner uncovered ancient manuscripts that spoke of cosmic elixirs and celestial transformations. Eldenport's residents immersed themselves in the cosmic texts, gaining insights into the alchemical processes that would unfold during the convergence. As the cosmic preparations intensified, the symbols on the ships emitted a radiant glow that resonated with the approaching celestial convergence. Eldenport's residents, now attuned to the cosmic symphony, felt the harmonious currents that surged through the town, creating a cosmic resonance that echoed through the universe. One celestial night, as Eldenport brimmed with celestial energies, the cosmic convergence manifested—a celestial vortex that pulsed with the rhythms of the universe. The symbols on the ships responded with a luminous display, marking the town as a focal point in the cosmic alchemy that would unfold. Eldenport sailed towards the cosmic convergence, guided by the symbols that now emanated a celestial sigil—an alchemical symbol representing the town's synthesis of Earthly and cosmic energies. The convergence loomed on the cosmic horizon, a celestial gateway to realms of cosmic transformation.

Eldenport sailed into the heart of the cosmic convergence, the symbols on the ships pulsating with the energies of celestial alchemy. The town's residents, now cosmic alchemists, embraced the transformative currents that enveloped Eldenport. As the cosmic convergence reached its zenith, a celestial radiance illuminated the town. Lila, Liam, Captain Sterling, and the elderly bookstore owner stood at the forefront, their beings resonating with the cosmic energies. The symbols, now integrated into their very essence, emitted a brilliant glow that mirrored the celestial forces at play. The celestial emissary appeared, its form transcending earthly definitions, a being of pure cosmic essence. It spoke through the symbols, conveying the culmination of Eldenport's cosmic journey—the town's evolution into a beacon of celestial harmony. The convergence became a cosmic stage where Earthly and celestial energies danced in unison. The symbols, now imbued with the essence of celestial alchemy, created intricate patterns that reflected the synthesis of the town's journey.

Eldenport's residents, surrounded by the celestial currents, felt a profound transformation. The cosmic elixir, a fusion of Earthly and celestial energies, coursed through their beings, unlocking latent potentials and expanding their consciousness. Lila's connection to cosmic energies deepened, Liam's artworks became portals to celestial realms, Captain Sterling gained an intuitive understanding of cosmic navigation, and the elderly bookstore owner became a living repository of cosmic wisdom. The celestial emissary conveyed a cosmic revelation—the town had become a celestial nexus, a place where Earthly and cosmic energies intertwined in perpetual harmony. Eldenport, now bathed in celestial light, stood as a testament to the cosmic possibilities that unfolded when communities embraced their cosmic destinies. The symbols on the ships, now radiating with the brilliance of celestial alchemy, became cosmic messengers. They carried Eldenport's cosmic story across the universe, inspiring other beings to explore the boundless connections between Earthly and celestial realms. As the cosmic convergence subsided, Eldenport sailed back through the cosmic currents, forever changed by the celestial alchemy it had experienced. The symbols, now an indelible part of the town's identity, continued to resonate through the universe.

About the Author

I have been wanting to write books for a while but never knew how. When writing a book, I always go with something random and don't always know what I want to write about. Sometimes there are a lot of different reasons for this, but for me personally, I just think of something random and go with it. There are times when I will use an AI to help me, but I was just messing around. I love how this book turned out and I hope you enjoy it.